THE AUTUMN TREE

THE AUTUMN TREE

Aysha Ehsan

Fresh Ink Group
Roanoke

THE AUTUMN TREE

Copyright © 2016

Fresh Ink Group
An Imprint of:
The Fresh Ink Group, LLC
PO Box 525
Roanoke, TX 76262
Email: info@FreshInkGroup.com
www.FreshInkGroup.com

Edition 1.1   2016

Book design by Ann E. Stewart

Cover by Mark Laxton / Stephen Geez

Cataloging-in-Publication Recommendations:
FIC000000 FICTION / General
FIC044000 FICTION / Contemporary Women
FIC062000 FICTION / Noir
FIC027020 FICTION / Romance / Contemporary

Library of Congress Control Number: 2016932469

ISBN-13: 978-1-936442-22-5

Dedication

"Behind every successful man there is a woman"—maybe!

But behind my success there are a woman and two men:

My lovely Mom & Dad,

And Asad.

Without your support, this was not possible.

To you all, with all my love.

Acknowledgements

The biggest supporters of my success have long been my lovely parents. Mama, thank you for your support, your advice, those loving scolding sessions, and for always being there for me. Papa, you are my hero, my first love, my mentor, and my life support. I love you two for making me the person I am.

My heartfelt gratitude goes to Fresh Ink Group for supporting my efforts. I would like to thank Stephen Geez for editing my simple autumn tree into a novel that makes me proud. Ann E. Stewart, those never-ending paragraphs look so good now because you put your talent into designing the layout of the book. Mark Laxton, hats off to you for your patience in designing the front cover, and to Stephen Geez for the back cover. And finally, thank you very much, Gary at Fresh Ink Group, for all your efforts in handling both me and *The Autumn Tree*. I'm sure it wasn't a new challenge for you because you seemed to handle it quite easily, but I am awed by the way you walked me through the entire process of publication. This has been my best experience ever!

Yours Sincerely

Chapter 1: Catherine

The show ended and end credits were running on the television screen, but Catherine hardly noticed. She was lost in her thoughts. Her reflections wandered through all her memories to recall the last time she had been carefree and comfortable. Even if any such memory came to light, it was so faint that she could not retain it. So much had happened since she moved to San Francisco. She had relocated from a small town to a big metropolis, dreaming of a wonderful future, a settled life, and a regular income. She knew very well there was no way back. Her mother had prohibited her from going away, but her dreams were too powerful to stop her. She never liked the life they lived. Nothing she wanted came into her possession. So she decided, following her instincts, to steal all her mother's savings, and boarded the bus to San Francisco.

She did not dare turn back.

It was not so much love for the town where she had spent her childhood, but the fear that someone might see her and force her to return. With her backpack under her seat, and hidden behind her novel, she prayed for the bus to leave town quickly. She stole the last glimpse of her hometown from just above the cover of her book, as sunlight was touching the tips of the trees to announce the beginning of a new day.

Eight months had passed since then. Catherine's passion and vigor dwindled with every passing month. Her fantasy of living in a high-class neighborhood had faded quickly as she faced the real world. The big city brought even bigger challenges. Her initial two months had been spent serving tuna, shrimp, lobster, and chowder in a restaurant down her street, where she lived in Fisherman's Wharf. She tried to interact with the tourists to show how talented she was, and that she should be swept off her feet and taken to the elegance of Berkeley. However, her efficiency ticked off the other waitresses, and within two days they got rid of her, effortlessly. Her next step lasted only three weeks. As a sales girl she was caught lost in her own world, staring at the fashionable couture, rather than presenting it to the customers. That had been tolerated, but getting caught sneaking into some of the newly arrived fashions proved fatal. This took her back to an increasingly wild search for any job at all. She had been struggling for the past three months without luck. Her patience had evaporated. She could not bear it anymore. The only option was going back home, and she had made her decision. How would she respond to all those questions and complaints about leaving unannounced and returning the same way? She could hear those mocking laughs of neighbors when they would see that she had come back home, defeated. Suddenly she felt suffocated, desperate to leave the narrow confines of her shabby room to breathe deeply in open air.

Catherine wrapped her shawl around her shoulders and, slipping into her flip-flops, quietly stepped out the door. The night air sent chills down her spine. She began to walk aimlessly. A group of young boys and girls were enjoying the evening. She envied their carefree lives. Did they know what complexities life had saved for them? Catherine felt it was her responsibility to advise them, to warn them about their forthcoming difficulties. She walked towards them, but all the kids hopped into a car and drove away, leaving a flyer to entertain her. Catherine would have ignored the piece of paper, but the eye-catching word *Free!* caught her attention. Retrieving it from the ground, she read it slowly. It touted a karaoke night at Pirate's Pub with free booze--an invitation to celebrate her last night in San Francisco. She headed to the venue.

Pirate's Pub looked nothing like she imagined. It appeared very classy, with everyone clad in brand-name clothing. How could rich people look good even with broken hearts? Taking her glass of Heineken, she settled into a corner and observed her surroundings. She belonged here, not fleeing back to her old small-town life. This was all for her, too, and she would do anything to be part of this scene. Catherine was lost in her fantasies when a girl screamed. Some gentlemen rushed to the other corner of the room. With the crowd around, she could not see the screaming lady, but the swearing and sobs clearly signaled that someone was extremely hurt.

Catherine watched the mayhem continue another twenty minutes. The young lady did not stop crying, so the opportunistic gentlemen gave up and left her on her own. She had buried her face in her hands and was shaking uncontrollably. Catherine sat next to her, careful not to further upset her as she cautiously placed a hand on her knee. The lady suddenly looked up. She was young, about Catherine's age. Mascara dripped down her cheeks, and her wavy mahogany hair looked ruffled, but she still appeared breathtakingly beautiful. Who could hurt such a gorgeous diva? When their eyes met, Catherine gave her a reassuring smile and said, "Don't worry, everything will be all right."

The diva stared at her in disbelief. She whispered without expression: "Nothing can ever be all right." Tears streamed down her cheeks as if all her inner barricades had broken. Catherine reached for her hand and squeezed it. The sad eyes rose again and searched Catherine's face. Then she started talking. "He will die, I tell you. He will die, and there in front of him will be his daughter, lying, the way I was, helpless." For the next few seconds she fell silent. Then her face contorted with disgust and the coming seconds brought another wave of swearing, moaning, and distressed tears. Catherine slipped her arm around her waist and urged her onto her feet. Ignoring the stares from all directions, she marched the crying soul out of the packed pub into the fresh air.

Open air did have a positive effect, and her loud moaning faded into soft sobs. At a little distance, benches appeared close to an artificial lake. Catherine hastened towards one, quickly settled the lady on it, and slipped next to her. She wanted to comfort her, but did not even know her name. Before she could say or do anything, the young lady started sobbing again. Catherine wrapped her arm around her. Clinging to Catherine, the poor stressed-out soul cried until she had no energy left. Lowering her head to rest in Catherine's lap, she panted for some time, then suddenly jolted upright and landed on the other side of the bench, her head striking the arm rest with a loud thud.

Catherine reached out to help her, but was repaid with a push. "Go away. Leave me alone." This was enough to tick her off, but somewhere in those lovely eyes Catherine could not avoid seeing deep sorrow, and that kept her calm. She wanted to help. Rather than trying to get her to talk, Catherine pulled the lady to her feet and offered to take her home. Waving down a taxi, she asked, "Where do you live?"

She appeared not to be heavily drunk, as she was pretty firm on her feet, so it must have been her mental state that caused her behavior. The lady composed herself, took a deep breath, and gracefully responded, "I have been grateful for your assistance, but I can find my way home. Please do not worry about me. It's getting late; you should be heading home, too." She met Catherine's eyes with a weak smile.

Catherine squeezed her hand and said, "All right, if that's what you want."

A taxi arrived. The lady climbed into the back seat and directed the driver to head towards Palo Alto. Catherine realized where she was going and made a request. "It's getting late, and I might not get another cab at this hour, so would you mind if I ride with you and get dropped later?"

The reaction was a numb, "No problem."

The ride was silent. The distressed young lady leaned her head on the window and closed her eyes while Catherine stared at the beautiful villas and apartments and considered how lucky the people living here were. The taxi skirted the deserted streets and reached the romantic Golden Gate Bridge. Catherine's pulse was racing, and she could not help but feel the magnetism of the area ahead. Looking straight ahead, she visualized herself descending in Palo Alto, leaving this semi-conscious girl to go to her place in Fisherman's Wharf instead. As they approached the vicinity, the driver inquired where to go.

The lady replied in a weak voice. "Falcon Heights."

To Catherine's surprise, the driver did not ask for directions. Rather, he sped rapidly. In the next two minutes the taxi stopped at the entrance of a huge apartment building glistening with spotlights circling every floor. Crafted to give the appearance of carved wood, the building was also constructed with brown bricks patterned on the surface. Creepers clinging to the wrought iron of the hanging balconies gave it the perfect touch, suggesting life in peace right in the center of a busy world. Unable to control her admiration, Catherine let her mouth fall open, her eyes glistening. She did not notice when her companion got out of the cab until she saw her walking towards the entrance. She called to ask her name.

Without turning around, she said, "Amanda," and walked inside the building.

Catherine was embarrassed by such treatment, but to her relief the driver was too robotic to respond to anything but destination directions. She asked him to drive to the next stop, and the car zoomed off. The moment they exited the sophistication of Palo Alto, Catherine's attention shifted to the meter, where the fare was mounting with incredible speed. Her first impulse was to ask the driver to stop, but then she wondered how she would walk to her place at this hour in the middle of the night. So with eyes fixed on the meter, she started considering how she would pay the bill, which was very much over her budget by now, and she was nowhere closer to home. She could not think of anything she owned that could be given in exchange of the payment. Mind working at the speed of the mounting fare, she suddenly realized she was only left with one valuable possession, her mother's gold- plated pendant. She could not consider giving it away under any circumstances, but here she had no other option. Numb with depression that her only ticket to go back home would be lost to strangers, she cursed every moment that had brought her to this stage.

When the driver paused in front of her house, Catherine was close to tears. The meter signaled a bill of $88, more than her food budget for the entire month. Slowly she removed her chain and looked at the pendant for one last time. Stretching her arm out reluctantly towards the driver, she said in a low voice, "I do not have cash. Will it be possible for you to take this pendant instead?"

The driver stared at her, surprised—or maybe confused.

Before he could say anything, she quickly continued. "It's gold plated. You can get it verified. Otherwise I live here and you can come in the morning to get your money. I will arrange it by noon." Her mind raced in every direction to find any source that could fund her, but she failed.

On the other hand, the driver's expression shifted to annoyance. "Your ride already has been paid by your friend, ma'am. Now if you could please excuse me. It's getting late."

It took some time to register. This was unbelievable. Before this dream ended, Catherine quickly pulled back her arm and jumped out of the cab. She had not even closed the door completely when the cab rushed away, disappearing into the night.

Catherine's night passed in a haze. She had escaped losing her only connection with home. At her doorstep, she found a small present for the upcoming Christmas. Carrying it inside, she could not stop smiling. These were signs. Fate had finally planned to reward her patience. She could feel good times approaching. Floating to bed, she promised herself that she would meet Amanda to thank her for such generosity.

Instincts were telling her Catherine would start a new chapter in her life . . .

The chapter of money and success.

Chapter 2: Amanda

Amanda woke up with the trapped feeling again.

Her mind kept asking the same question: *How will I get this filth off me?* She wanted to scream, but did not have the energy to do it. She despised her state. She did not even have freedom of letting her feelings out. Her activities were scrutinized by him, her body would not support her to do what she wished, and her soul was bruised--damaged, then killed that unfortunate afternoon. She knew she was living, but dead inside. The torment continued, and she felt disgusted every second. She clearly remembered those days when life seemed perfect. She could still visualize that passion, vigor, and spirit to succeed. At every step toward achieving her dream, she had Brad right beside her, supporting her, counseling her, and protecting her--except for that unfortunate day, the only day he did not guard her. That was the day she died, not even a month ago.

Amanda slipped out of her bed and walked towards the restroom. In a haze, she tripped over a pair of sandals, which she had removed and left in the middle of the room last night. Grabbing the arm of a chair, she balanced. She knew her usual reaction would have been a loud curse and a probable kick to anything in her way. Rather, she straightened and continued walking. Every bit inside her screamed, *You are dead!*

Back in the living room, she began preparing breakfast. Last night's commotion had stressed her mentally as well as physically. She felt hungry. Soaking some cereal in a bowl of milk, Amanda carried her breakfast to the couch and sat on her spot. Surfing through all the channels, she could not find anything interesting. She wondered why the broadcasting stations did not realize that weekends were the time when something good should be aired.

Giving up, she muted the television and started eating her breakfast. By the fifth bite, her cellphone buzzed, notifying her of an instant message. Right then she lost her appetite. The bite in her mouth felt like paper. She knew who it was. Ignoring the sound, she started mixing the cereal vigorously to control her shaking body. When nothing else happened, she started to calm down. It took some time for her heartbeat to revert to its normal rate, and then there was peace.

Just then the doorbell rang and startled. She had never had guests at her place, and was certainly not expecting anyone. She almost dropped the bowl, spilling some of the paste on her pajamas. Regaining composure, she tidied herself and headed towards the door. Who could possibly be there? When she opened the door, she encountered the same young lady who had paraded her out of the pub last night. Amanda was in no mood to welcome her, but courtesy called for a decent gesture, so she returned her bright smile with a nod. Both stood on each side of the door in an awkward silence until Amanda realized that the lady was expecting to be invited in. Opening the door slightly more, she gestured her unwanted guest in with a forced smile. "Please come in."

*   *   *

Catherine could feel that she was not welcome, but she acted as if she did not know. Entering the apartment, she scanned it with obvious admiration. This place was exactly like she had always imagined her house after becoming successful. The comfy brown couch facing the huge high-end TV sat a perfect distance from the balcony. The wall behind it was decorated with a randomly hanging set of three decorations, which were multicolored and three-dimensional. The plush carpet felt soft beneath her worn-out shoes. The wooden chimes hanging above the exit towards the balcony complimented the peach-and-brown abstract wallpaper on that single wall. Opposite, an open kitchen displayed some very elegant crockery placed neatly. Catherine could not stop admiring the place. When she finally turned back to look at her host, she noticed a magnificent cross nailed right above the door. This religious depiction impressed her.

Clearly annoyed by this unannounced guest and her boldness, Amanda asked, "What brings you here?

*   *   *

Looking rather taken aback by the bluntness, Catherine recovered and replied with a smile. "I thought I should check on you. You were not in a very good state last night."

"I'm sure you knew very well that I was all right." Amanda was deliberately being rough so this intruder would get the message to leave her alone.

But this lady seemed adamant to stay. Rather, she complained, "Is that how you treat your guests?"

Amanda suddenly felt ashamed. Her mother would have been very stressed if she saw how she treated her visitor, so she gave up her coldness and apologized. Then she invited the lady to sit and make herself comfortable. She went into the kitchen to fetch a glass of orange juice. Her visitor began acting as if they were old friends. She complimented in a surprisingly loud tone that Amanda's home looked beautiful. Not knowing how to react, Amanda remained silent and barely smiled. Carrying the glass, she walked around the kitchen counter and reached the couch slowly. When she handed the glass over, her visitor gave a wide smile and continued chatting. "By the way, I'm Catherine."

Amanda was not interested, which she displayed with silence. Catherine ignored her again. She sipped the juice and seemed to enjoy its taste thoroughly. Amanda grew perplexed that Catherine did not get the signals she was giving. To her surprise, she even asked where Amanda worked. The question disturbed her so immensely that she suddenly got up. She had been trying every possible way since she woke up not to think about him, yet now all the ugly memories flooded back. She curtly directed Catherine, "I am busy, and can you please leave?"

Amanda's abrupt reaction shook Catherine, so she tried to pacify the environment. "Umm, but what--" She had not yet completed what she was saying when Amanda reached the door. Opening it wide, she waited for Catherine to leave.

Catherine stood up and walked straight to the door.

*   *   *

When Catherine stepped into the corridor, Amanda closed the door immediately behind her. Catherine walked slowly towards the elevator. While she was waiting for it to open, her mind raced over all the potential opportunities she had observed in the apartment. She was still admiring the decoration, but her mind stuck on the notebook placed on the center-table in the living room. Its cover page displayed a pencil sketch of a building. On top of the black-and-white page, two words in bold attracted attention:

Immaculate University

Underneath the bold letters, a tiny lettered statement in italics supported it:

Our Destination Is Success!

Catherine floated her way down, out of the building. A pleasant walk with a nice breeze added joy to her mood. She knew that her *Destination is success,* too.

Her next visit would be to Immaculate University.

Chapter 3: Brad

He was a success story.

At the age of eighteen, he had plunged into the stock market and, with smartness and charisma, multiplied his small investments. Reinvestments into property, a personal website, and a successful private consultancy made him a millionaire-entrepreneur by the age of thirty-two. Brad Orwell enjoyed every moment of his life. Even when he failed to qualify for the best business school because he could not tell the GDP of the United States during the interview, his disappointment continued exactly one and a half hours. A call from his nearly forgotten ex led to an elegant buffet dinner at The Ritz, followed by passionate love-making in the back seat of his car. By the time he dropped her, he had completely forgotten about the interview—and the GDP of the U.S.

No woman could escape the charms of this handsome young man whose innocent eyes and seductive smile proved an irresistible combination. Once he deployed these weapons, any woman he wanted fell under his spell. The final magic would come from his humor, which was always calculated.

Hooking up the innocent red-haired beauty was easy. He did not even have to put in any effort because she was already crazy about him. Every evening she came to the coffee shop adjacent his office and ordered tea. The moment he walked into the shop, she would stiffen with evident anxiety. She would stare at him constantly, but the moment he would turn to look at her she would look away, turning *the bitch mode* on— unsuccessfully. The scarlet of her burning cheeks would always betray her, revealing how she must be shaking inside.

He could never forget the evening he approached her. Tired of the teenage hide-and-seek, he walked straight to her in the shop and casually asked, "So you're buying me coffee, right?" The poor girl was shocked out of her seat and almost spilled her tea, but he admired how she covered her shock.

Obviously faking a seductive attitude, she managed a smile and with shaky voice said, "I won't mind, you can order." Her sparkling eyes and beaming face gripped his heart instantly, just as it has ever since. He enjoyed how she stuttered her name with excitement, "Am—Am—

Amanda!"

Brad had enjoyed relationships with many women, but Amanda became both a friend and a partner simultaneously. He approached her with the aim of showing a pretty girl heaven in life, but instead got himself carried away by a deeper relationship.

Amanda was a strong, independent young lady, passionate to become a successful professional. He enjoyed supporting her ambitions by occasionally advising and sometimes counseling her. Sharing everything new and old with him, she would be satisfied only when she had reported anything happening in her life. Every time she shared her adventures, her eyes sparkled and she shivered with excitement until she would complete the story. Then she would sigh with relief and immediately drop down, laying her head on his lap and talking dreamily to herself, creating various crazy endings to the current story. She would absently play with his goatee or his shirt's button.

He knew very well that Amanda was an introvert, so he always encouraged her to talk. What he really enjoyed about her was that she would understand things with a slight delay. Every time she got into any argument or heated-up situation, she would not understand what to do. Then later she would reenact the whole scenario with a favorable ending. During such a catharsis he would support her by sitting quietly and listening.

Their relationship had succeeded for almost two years now, and never in all this time had he seen Amanda so lost and solemn. Over the past month her spark had vanished, and on many occasions perhaps her thoughts became so loud that she did not listen to him.

Today was another such day. In the hour since he arrived, she had not said a word other than a casual greeting. She was lying on the couch, her head on his lap, but she was not all there. He got no reaction when he rubbed her hair, switched the channels, or shifted position a couple of times just to get her attention. When nothing worked, he started talking about the movie playing on the screen.

"I wonder why Gayle Gere did not leave her for what she did. I guess no man can tolerate his wife giving him horns." He shifted his gaze to her face, expecting her response.

Amanda glanced at the screen, but froze when she saw that the movie playing was *Unfaithful*. Her heart was beating fast. She clenched his shirt tightly and fought back tears. Brad felt her discomfort and stroked her hair. When he turned her face toward him, he was shocked to see tears streaming down the side. He immediately pulled her up and hugged her tightly. He had never seen her so disoriented. He held her until she stopped shaking.

When their eyes finally met, she asked in a low voice, "What if the woman did not do it voluntarily? What if there was no other option?"

Brad looked at Amanda for a few seconds, then burst into laughter. "Since when did you start taking movies so seriously? I talked about it so I could get your attention, but you are talking nonsense." When he saw that Amanda was uncomfortable, he backed off, which was not easy because these were the moments when he would tease her and she would argue with all her silly stances that he would strike down in rapid fire. Finally she would be so flustered that she would grab him and start kissing him hard until he wouldn't be able to laugh.

Today, rather than fighting back, Amanda got even more defensive. This raised Brad's concern. Pulling her into his embrace, he tried to calm her down. Amanda melted into his arms and clutched his wrists like a child. Kissing her hair lightly, its scent redolent of watermelon shampoo, he trailed his nose down her neck and along her right shoulder. Slowly tightening his grip around her waist, he kissed her neck until he reached her chin, then turned her around his lips. His lips touched Amanda's. She was growing warmer. Slightly rubbing the lower part of her bosom, he kissed her hard on the mouth. Amanda started to ease with each new touch. Feeling encouraged he slowly moved her on the couch and climbed on top of her. Amanda's hand moved up, and she grabbed his hair. He could feel her excitement, and this thrilled him even more. He was finally reaching the lively passionate Amanda he adored.

Thrilled by these actions, he slipped his hands under her waist and hip and continued kissing wildly. Grabbing her hair tight he pulled her face roughly and sucked her neck so hard that she screamed. This exhilarated him even more. He quickly unbuttoned her blouse and, cupping her breast, he began sucking.

Within seconds Amanda had gone completely cold and stopped reacting. It seemed as if that invisible shield had again taken her over. He lifted his head to look closer. Amanda's eyes were wide open and she was staring at the ceiling. It seemed as if he were taking advantage of her. He felt disgusted. Immediately he moved away and sat straight. Amanda's reaction proved even more disturbing. She quietly buttoned her blouse and sat next to him. Brad searched her face for any of that connection they had shared for so long. He saw a blank face—a face absolutely plain—with eyes hard as stone. Amanda had never been so cold. It bothered him to see such hard eyes on the soft and innocent face of this girl who had always brought a smile to his own. He wished he could reach deep inside her and squeeze out what had been bothering her. But she would not allow him.

He had no idea how long they sat there just looking into each other's eyes. He tried slipping past the steel barricade, but nothing welcomed him. He was clueless as to what was going on inside Amanda. When she did not say anything, he slowly broke eye contact and stood up. Picking up his car keys, he managed a casual, "All right then, I'll be leaving now."

Amanda neither moved nor uttered a word. She only stared at him.

Bending down, he kissed her forehead and moved towards the door. A last glance at her made him uncomfortable. Her eyes appeared sad, but she was silent. He knew she should be given some time for herself.

Promising himself that he would get her out of this, he stepped out.

Chapter 4: Amanda

Please don't leave me alone!

Amanda was screaming inside.

Please listen to me! I would never want to betray your trust—but I had no other option."

The last time Brad had turned, she wanted to rush over and get lost in his embrace. She wanted to feel the protection he always gave her. Shrinking on the couch, she tightly hugged her legs. Amanda wanted to be free of this torture. She could not bear her soul's corrosion. She cried until her throat hurt, her eyes swelling so much that she couldn't focus her vision. She yearned to clean the filth left on her soul, and wanting only to be clean again for Brad.

She did not notice how long she cried. The light ringtone of her cellphone brought her back. She answered hoping it would be Brad.

Before she could say anything, the voice she abhorred barked, "You need to learn to be obedient. You are taking undue advantage of my lenience."

Amanda froze. She could picture his cruel face, the way he smiled wickedly while training her. His mocking laughter echoed in her ears even now. Amanda wanted to shut herself somewhere she could not be reached. He kept speaking.

When Amanda did not respond, he barked, "Do you hear me?" He was so loud, she had to move the phone away from her ear.

Unable to speak, Amanda started weeping. Her soft sobs halted his continuous rebuke. She hated that her weakness gave him a sense of power, that he would grow increasingly aroused with every trembling intake of her breath as he listened silently to the melodious sound of her crying. Sitting five kilometers away, he would feel his authority, and to him this was ecstasy.

When Amanda finally gained composure, that voice hissed, "So I should take it as affirmation for my invitation, right?" He made no effort to hide his annoyance at her silence. Between gritted teeth he ordered, "Be ready in half an hour; I want to display my prettiest prisoner." After a moment, he continued, "Wear a backless dress that shows most of your cleavage. Like I said, I want to display you. I'm sure you won't disappoint me. After all, you do not want your parents to receive your nude pictures." Finally, that voice that still held so much power over her disconnected with a self-satisfied chuckle.

Amanda's tears eventually dried. She had been crying so much since that unfortunate afternoon that now, even if she tried, she could not.

*   *   *

Twelve storeys down in the parking lot, Brad grew impatient in his Porsche 911. He wondered what was bothering Amanda. They had always respected each other's privacy, and he did not want to intrude upon hers. He hoped she would confide in him one day, and he wished that day would come soon.

Driving out of the parking lot, he stole a glance at Amanda's apartment, and he missed the way she was always lingered there on her balcony, seeing him off.

She was not there.

Chapter 5: Catherine

Catherine sealed the envelope and scribbled her name in bold on the front. While she underlined the name, the folds of her résumé ended under the pen, and it pierced through the envelope. Catherine cursed herself for such carelessness. "Going to the Immaculate University, and just *look* at the level of your perfection," she muttered under her breath. She tried to smooth the paper, but it got worse, so she gave up and left it the way it was. This was her last piece of stationery, and she had clearly spoiled it out of anxiety.

She spread her pants on the bed and examined them. They were creased and slightly torn on the belt. She would cover it by pulling the top down. Her cotton floral blouse with a white base was not at all a match with the black trousers, but she had no other choice. Her shoes were worn out, but she polished them until they looked presentable.

Once she had prepared for the next morning, she went to the kitchen for dinner. With the only food available, she settled for with a cup of sugar-free green tea and some crackers. The more she realized how she was surviving, the more she got frustrated. She recalled Amanda's apartment and envied her luck. She wished she could live her life. Her grandmother always said, "B*e careful what you wish for, you might get it!*" Catherine smiled at the thought and said out loud, "I wish I get to live the life Amanda lives."

A sense of satisfaction spread all inside her.

Chapter 6: Matheus

Exactly half an hour later, Matheus cruised in his SUV right in front of the entrance to Falcon Heights.

This was an impressive part of town, and he appreciated Amanda's taste. He had always considered her to be an upright, passionate young lady who did not compromise on reputation. He knew she belonged to a well-established family and was only working for fun. He still remembered how long it took to bring her inside his office. Even training took more time than usual. At one point he had even felt that she would walk out, but that threat about her boyfriend had stopped her. He had never experienced this before, but he admitted that day that he was worried his bluff might be exposed. He smiled at the thought of how love can blind us to reality. She loved that man so much that she had agreed to submit. And then he had trained her, a training so meticulous that when she walked out of his office she was completely a different person.

He was still taking pleasure from his triumph when Amanda walked out from the building. His smile faded when he saw her wearing a long black gown, which covered from her shoulders right down to her toes. On top of it, she had wrapped a blue stole around her shoulders, covering her beautiful bosom completely from view. Climbing in the car, she sat expressionless, looking out the window. He had to admit that she was a beautiful young lady. She had not applied any make-up. This was obviously deliberate, so he was ready for this challenge. Amanda had done everything contrary to his desires.

Controlling his temper, he managed a statement in a single tone: "I asked you to wear something sensual. Why are you dressed like a widow? I see you're not wearing makeup, either. You know I am very fond of it."

Amanda was mute. She seemed like a statue sitting next to him.

He was fuming by now. Grabbing her arm, he turned her to face him. When their eyes met, he saw wrath in her eyes, as if fire was placed in the hollows of eyes on a face carved out of stone. She didn't try to hide her hatred. This provoked him further, and he felt himself getting hard. At his age, Viagra took even more time to show its effects, but Amanda's disgust for him stimulated his sense of power and authority. His lips curved into a mocking smile.

It was triumph.

He had succeeded in making her feel intensely about him.

*   *   *

Amanda was disgusted by this man who was clearly suffering from arrested adolescence. How could he be comfortable knowing that she despised him? She wanted to scream out that she hated him. His evil face looked even worse when he tried to smile. An attack of Bell's Palsy had left the lower left half of his face numb, apart from occasional sensations. But when that part of his face did move, it made him seem the true embodiment of Satan, and that was such a night. His abnormal twitch accompanied by hollow laughter filled the SUV.

After enjoying the moment for a long stretch, he looked ahead and spoke in a relaxed tone. "We are not going anywhere. You look exhausted. It would be better that you relax."

Amanda was baffled. She could not believe what she was hearing. She had never expected sympathy from this animal.

She was only trying to digest what he had said when he continued, "I would also like to relax, but the Viagra I took before coming is disturbing me."

A chill swept over Amanda. She did not want him to touch her. When he leaned towards her, she shrank back. His hand rubbed her thigh and she slapped it away. He was now enjoying his chase.

Amanda hated the way she always seemed to give him pleasure in the hunt.

*   *   *

After she repelled several of his attempts, he sat back and relaxed. Lighting his cigar, he took a long puff. Blowing the smoke into her face, he played with a strand of her mahogany-hued hair. From the holder on the door, he picked up a manila envelope and examined it. He could feel Amanda getting tense. Not shifting his gaze from the parcel in his hand, he spoke in a low voice. "How much time do you think it will take for a parcel to get from here to New York City? I can deliver this to your special friend, if you wish."

Amanda looked like a trapped rabbit surrounded by wolves. Her expression aroused him even more. This was getting better and better.

"You have probably forgotten the memories of that wonderful afternoon we first spent together. Let me refresh your memory." Opening the envelope, he slid out a stack of photographs.

Amanda closed her eyes.

He looked at the pictures for some time, then placed three on Amanda's lap. "Look at them," he ordered her. Slipping his hand behind her neck he squeezed it and repeated the command between gritted teeth.

Amanda squealed with pain. She looked down at the pictures of herself that she had never been able to accept. This was not the first time she had seen these photographs, and he counted on each time the pain getting worse. Tears were flowing down her cheeks as she sat there, defeated again.

When he was sure that she had completely submitted, he slipped his hand down her neck. He made some attempts to arouse her but it seemed impossible. Amanda was a challenge.

Since he could not make her respond, he did what he was good at: satisfy his own twisted needs regardless of another's pain.

*   *   *

The watchman wondered what was going on behind the black windows of the huge SUV. It had been twenty minutes since the pretty woman from 1207 climbed in it. She was a friendly lady who always acknowledged him and asked how he felt. Recently she had seemed lost and sad. Her friend who drove a Porsche had already left. She had never gone in any car other than the Porsche or her own. This seemed to be new twist.

What he could make out from the movement of shadows was nothing promising--until the driver suddenly sprang onto the lady. This got the watchman feeling excited. As the SUV started bouncing, his hand moved towards his zipper. Holding himself from above the trousers, he began rubbing.

The SUV bounced up and down, and with it he also synchronized his rhythm. The vehicle finally stopped after five minutes.

By then he was ready to pay a visit to the restroom.

*   *   *

Amanda's soul died once again.

He was lying on top of her and panting heavily. Amanda had not felt anything but self-disgust. When he slipped off her, she slowly sat up, got dressed, opened the door, and left without a word.

"You can take a rest for the whole week. There is no need for you to come in," he said.

She shut the door while he was in the middle of saying something, then walked back in the entrance and up to the elevator.

She was in such a haze that nothing around her seemed real.

*   *   *

The watchman came back to his seat and realized that the lady from 1207 was waiting for the elevator. She seemed to be lost. The elevator opened twice for her to enter, but she did not move. He wondered what she was thinking.

He walked to her and spoke in a teasing tone. "Ma'am, your ride is waiting for you."

Rather than going inside, she looked at the watchman. Her eyes were full of sadness. There was not even a fraction of excitement that he could find in her.

She seemed to be searching for something on his face, and then came a flood of tears.

He was clueless as to what should be done. He just stood there, looking at her. What happened in the car must not have been what she wanted. He felt disgusted at himself for his thinking and actions. He had been taking pleasure in what he was looking at, but now seeing the reality was disturbing.

The lady composed herself and stepped inside the elevator.

When the elevator closed, he realized he was observing a strong lady who stood straight and firm.

But the tears depicted how broken she was.

Chapter 7: Catherine

Immaculate University was in the "International Education Cluster" (IEC). Its campus was almost half of the "Aristotle Cluster" of IEC. Catherine was thrilled to see the dynamism of the campus. The building's front was made of tinted glass, which reflected its logo: a gold star flashing and leaving behind light and brightness.

As she stepped into the reception area, the black marble floor sparkled with embedded glittering specks. The walls were textured in beige. The reception had a huge waiting lounge with four sets of couches placed near each corner of the room. In the middle of the lounge sat a large 3D model of the flashing star. The reception desk was opposite the entrance. Catherine crossed the logo and walked straight to it. The students and staff members were all fashionably dressed. She was excited to be present in such refined ambience.

Two young and gorgeous receptionists greeted everyone. They were dressed in navy-blue business suits with crisp white shirts. Both had their hair tied in neat buns, and the gold star shone on their jackets as a badge.

When Catherine approached the desk, they were already attending to some people. She waited patiently for her turn.

When one of them got free, she turned to Catherine with a bright smile. "How may I help you?" she asked in a pleasant tone.

"I—I came to drop my résumé, please," Catherine stammered with anxiety. Extending her hand, she handed over the punctured envelope.

The lady read her name and responded in a proper-but-monotonic tone. "Ms. Catherine, your résumé will be forwarded to the Human Resources Department, and you will receive a call when there is a vacancy. Thank you."

This obviously meant that she should leave, but Catherine did not move.

The lady continued to smile for Catherine, but when she noticed that she was not planning to move, she aimlessly started sifting through the papers in front of her.

Getting the signal, Catherine began to move. An idea struck her. "Can I please see my résumé? I need to add something."

The young lady handed her envelope back with the same smile.

Taking it, Catherine asked for a pen. She was handed a red pen, which she did not appreciate much, but she had no choice. Underneath her name she scribbled, *c/o Amanda.*

Returning the résumé, she turned back slowly and headed towards the doors. She wanted to wander around and see the whole place, but was conscious of being scrutinized. Therefore, she left the campus right away.

Once on the road, she waved down a passenger bus and climbed aboard. Her mind was still in the impressive ambience. She prayed silently that she would at least be called for an interview. She would do anything to prove that she would work hard.

Catherine was engrossed in her prayers when her phone rang. It took some time to locate the phone in her handbag. When she finally retrieved it, it was not ringing. It indicated a missed call from an unknown number. She wondered if she should call back. Within a minute the same number called again.

"Hello!" she said in a pleasant tone.

"Hello. Am I speaking to Ms. Catherine Smith?" inquired a male voice.

"Speaking," Catherine confirmed.

"Ma'am, I am Dr. Anthony Hopkins from Immaculate University. I just received your résumé. Is it possible for you to meet me right now?"

*   *   *

Dr. Hopkins did not get any response. Maybe he'd taken her breath away. He inquired, "Are you there?"

This was awkward. He already had a deadline from the president of the university, and now this promising candidate was either too dumbstruck or too busy to respond to his call. He could feel she was listening to him but, surprisingly, she was quiet. He asked one final time if she was there.

Then came an exasperated burst. "Yes please, sir. I—I, yes, sir, this is Catherine Smith—" After a small pause: "—speaking."

Anthony's lip curled up with his suspicious signature smile. His mustache touched his lip, tickling him. The tickle was intense because he could feel that he had finally reached his target. Now was his turn to be silent and wait for the lady to get frustrated.

She was breathing heavily, but finally spoke. "Sir, this is Catherine Smith. I dropped my résumé at Immaculate University."

Her emphasis on "I" told him how desperate she was for a job. The disturbing storm inside him started to settle. Pleasantly he thought, *Hop-*

kins, you are a master of intuition.

When Sebastian had handed him the unimpressive envelope, he did not notice it at first. The hurried scribble of Amanda's name tempted him to call this lady. He surely did not regret making this move. He winked at Sebastian.

Sebastian's lip twitched slightly, but his face remained expressionless.

*   *   *

On the other end of the line, Catherine was now shaking with desperation. She wondered why the gentleman was not speaking. She checked the cellphone screen to confirm the connection was receiving signal. Everything was perfect.

When she brought the phone near her ear again, the gentleman was already speaking. "Today, will it be possible for you?"

Catherine did not have any idea what he was saying. She could not let go of this chance. She stammered, "Sir, could you—can you please repeat?"

The gentleman paused, then spoke with authority. "Will it be possible for you to visit me in my office today? We have some vacancies to be filled urgently."

Barely able to control her excitement, she responded cheerfully, "Sure, sir, absolutely. Should I come right now?"

He responded in a casual tone. "Hmmm . . . All right, come over. I will be in a meeting the whole afternoon. Inform the reception that you are here for interview in my office."

"Thank you, sir. Thank you. I am on my way. God bless."

Catherine was too excited. When the call disconnected, she realized that everyone on the bus was staring at her. She had been too loud.

Composing, herself she waited for the next bus stop. The moment the bus halted, she sprang to her feet and bounced out. Just in a couple of leaps she was on the other side of the road and waiting for another bus to take her to Immaculate University.

*   *   *

Anthony was surprised by her reaction. Fortunately she saved him the time of setting the stage, of making it sound like he was calling from a very professional work place.

She was ready to come.

Now was the time to pin down the prey.

*   *   *

Stepping into the reception lounge, Catherine felt confident. Two hours ago when she had entered the same entrance she was defensive and needy. Now the conditions were different, and so was her gait.

She approached the receptionist with poise and declared, "I have an appointment with Dr. Anthony." She did shake a bit because she did not remember his complete name, but that passed quickly because the receptionist immediately recognized the name.

With the same artificial smile, she responded, "Yes, Ms. Catherine Smith, please have a seat. Dr. Hopkins is in a meeting at the moment. You will be called in shortly."

Catherine walked to the closest couch and sat. She observed the huge lounge. It impressed no less than any grand hotel. Two large corridors on each side of the reception desk led into dimly lit passages. Beside the corridors, two immense staircases curled up to the upper floor. All the lecture halls and cafeteria on the first floor had glass walls, and what was going on in there could be seen. Groups of students huddled and chatted at various stops in the larger cafeteria. Some lecture halls were vacant, and some had classes in progress. The architecture of the building was exquisite. The ceiling above the reception lounge went up to the top of the first floor. Four elegant chandeliers hung from the ceiling right above each set of couches. So engrossed in her observation, she was startled to find one of the receptionists standing right next to her.

"Ms. Smith, you can go in. Mr. Sebastian will guide." She gestured towards the passage to the left of the reception desk.

A strongly built man with suspicious expression stood at the start of the passage, waiting for Catherine. His gaze made her uncomfortable. She had noticed him on her initial visit, too. He was continually looking around, murmuring into a Bluetooth headset. Mr. Sebastian looked like a spy.

Pushing aside all these thoughts, she walked confidently towards him. She had not yet reached him when he turned and started walking into the passage. It took Catherine a couple of leaps to match his brisk pace. They were moving too fast for her to read any of the names on the doors. The passage was a complete opposite of the glass castle outside. This was dimly lit and fully carpeted, its walls colored with wood-brown paint. All the doors were black with gold knobs and gold name plates showing names etched in black.

Near the end, Mr. Sebastian paused. Continually murmuring, he opened the door on the right and stepped in. The name on the door said:

Dr. Anthony Hopkins, PhD
Administrative Vice-Chancellor

Catherine's confidence grew as she realized that the top-tier official of the university had called her in after seeing her résumé. Memorizing the name, she followed the murmuring man. The soft carpet from the passage continued inside the office. The room was very well furnished with teak-wood furniture. In the middle sat a large desk that had sheets of paper placed neatly near the far end. A miniature flag with the university logo rested on the other end. Two comfortable chairs in front of the desk had a small square table between them. A separate table in the corner behind the desk held a coffee percolator, a pack of Britannia Digestive Biscuits, one container each of walnuts and almonds, Nescafe, and creamer. As Catherine looked with astonishment, her belly growled, complaining that it had not been fed since morning.

Looking away from the refreshments, she focused with disappointment on the bald gentleman on a large brown office chair. Dr. Anthony was nothing like what she imagined. The way he had talked on the phone encouraged her, but standing there in his office she felt her heart sinking. Dr. Hopkins did not seem to be in a good mood. His face was naturally impious with a moustache grown until almost inside his mouth. His gaze was absolutely discomforting, and he was frowning so deeply that his face contorted, pulling up his cheeks, partially closing the eyes. He did not seem to be pleased with Catherine's visit. She definitely did not have the strength for another disappointment. Tension sent chills through her body, giving her goose bumps.

This is not how she imagined this meeting.

Chapter 8: Anthony

This was not the girl Anthony imagined.

Seeing Amanda's name on the envelope, he'd guessed that her referral would be pretty—if not stunning. But the young lady who entered was not anywhere close to the category. She was around five feet five, with a very *unimpressive* figure. Shoulders slumped forward made her breasts hang. The ill-fitting trousers played the remaining part of ruining her appearance.

Nothing about her was provocative. Above all, her obvious self-consciousness made her look too vulnerable. The way she was scanning from one corner to the other annoyed him. Just in the initial ten seconds, Anthony decided to turn her down.

But her gait emitted desperation. Now this looked promising! So Anthony decided to give it a shot.

Bending forward, he gestured towards the seat opposite him.

The young woman moved abruptly, which showed how desperate she was. She could barely control her excitement and trembling hands.

"In what capacity did Ms. Goldsmith refer you to this university?"

Instead of responding, she looked completely lost.

Anthony was greatly annoyed. *Not again,* he thought. When she did not seem to gather anything, he asked, "Ms. Goldsmith recommended you?"

Catherine looked at him as if expecting him to continue.

When she did not say anything, he repeated, "You mentioned that Ms. Amanda Goldsmith sent you—"

She obviously had no ready answer. "Amanda, Amanda—ummm—Amanda is a friend, a very good friend."

Anthony figured she did not even know Amanda. This would be easy now. To further exasperate her, he declared, "Ms. Smith, our university has been set up on the basis of truth and professionalism. I can see that you do not know Ms. Amanda—even though you claim that you do."

This was enough to stress her. He enjoyed seeing the way she clutched the arm of the seat and moved to the edge of it. She tried to make a desperate attempt to convince him. "But, sir, I—I—I will work very hard. I'll do anything to prove that I can be a good choice. Please give me one chance—just one chance."

Anthony was amused. His attempt was right on target. When he was sure that Catherine was completely defeated, he said, "My child, I can see that you are a determined and a passionate young lady, but our rules cannot be compromised. We in Immaculate University are like a family, and our first obligation is to be truthful."

Highly embarrassed, she clearly did not know what to do. She had realized her mistake. Not controlling the commotion inside her, she started crying.

Anthony already did not find Catherine attractive, and the way her face twisted while crying completely turned him off. But the idea that she was ready to do anything to get this job kept him hooked up.

He stood up and walked around the desk to approach her. Placing a gentle hand on her shoulder, he calmed her down. Waving Sebastian to leave, he took the seat opposite her.

When she seemed to calm down, he continued, "You are surely a dynamic person, and I can guarantee that you will do wonders if you are employed."

He paused to check if she was following him, and she was.

"Child, here we work very close together. Anything we say or do is closely watched. Our president stays updated with every aspect of the university."

By now, Catherine was stable and listening to him with concentration, but the deadly silence of the room was suddenly broken by a loud growl from her belly. Catherine seemed embarrassed.

He felt it was the right time to snare her in the net. Hungry and desperate were the best qualities in a prey.

He walked over to the refreshment corner and switched on the coffee percolator, then decorated a small plate with two biscuits and a large quantity of nuts. Adding creamer to a steaming cup of coffee, he turned slightly and asked, "Sugar?"

Catherine responded nervously. "Yes, please, two."

He stirred in the sugar, place the mug and plate on the table and settled opposite her. "I suspect you are in dire need of a job. I think I can help you."

Catherine's face lit up.

And he knew he was capturing her. He could practically hear her heart beating very fast. She had felt ashamed of herself for lying, but by now would be thankful that he was such a thoughtful gentleman. He had seen beyond her excuse. He had looked into her soul . . .

Yes, here sat a woman who thought herself capable of doing wonders, someone who only needed one chance to prove it. Catherine was now seeing an angel behind the naturally crooked face.

Anthony had achieved enough acceptance and respect in her heart to further be generous and win it all over. He asked her to eat something because he could see she was hungry.

Still a bit awkward, Catherine took a bite of the dry biscuit. She struggled to swallow until she sipped the steaming coffee. Looking pleased with the flavors, she devoured the large biscuit in two more bites. Then she munched some walnuts along with the coffee. She was eating her nervousness away. When she finished the whole plate, she finally managed an eye contact with Dr. Hopkins.

He offered her his best pleasant smile.

Catherine had turned out to be an easy target. Now, how could she be made presentable for the president? She had natural assets to be feasted upon, including her swelling breasts. When she looked at him her eyes sparkled and she looked better. He just needed to make her more comfortable. "Tell me all about yourself."

Catherine hesitated a bit, but relaxed and started sharing her problems with him. She spoke about her challenges and struggles. She explained how she had been trying hard to get a job, then met Amanda by accident, a lucky accident that brought her to this place. By the time she ended, she was grinning from ear to ear.

Smiling warmly, Anthony said, "You are a promising young lady. I will discuss your case with the president and set your interview. You should go home and take some rest now. Come back to meet me tomorrow at 4 p.m. I'll personally introduce you to the president."

And he won her over.

She would thank God enough for His blessings. She was shivering with excitement.

She stood and flashed a bright smile. "Thank you, Dr. Hopkins. Thank you. I have no other words to express how grateful I am."

Anthony responded with a smile, then reached into his pocket and produced a $50 bill. Extending it to her, he said, "Please buy a neat business suit and be very presentable tomorrow. Our president is very particular about attire. After all, we are the family of Immaculate University. Look your best and I guarantee that I will give you all my support."

Anthony had become her guardian angel. Catherine's gratitude spilled down her check in tears. Taking the money, she whispered, "May God bless you always."

He walked her to the door and saw her out.

God bless me, indeed.

Chapter 9: Catherine

Catherine was too emotional to notice anyone on her way out. With food in her stomach and money in her pocket, the world seemed a better place.

She stopped at a shop that sold second-hand clothes at very reasonable prices. She was their regular customer. She picked a pair of black trousers and a matching jacket. To complement the suit, she selected an orange blouse. The bill for these items was $22.99, so she dropped the idea of getting new shoes.

Walking home after shopping, she stopped for a pack of sausages, bread, 3-in-1 coffee packets, and a hotdog. Everything seemed different and much more pleasant. Catherine smiled at everyone she passed.

Entering her building, she walked straight up to her neighbor Susan's apartment and rang the bell. Susan looked surprised at Catherine's cheerful demeanor. It had been months since Catherine had smiled, and here she was beaming. Susan looked stunned when she noticed the bags in her hand. Catherine looked like she had won the lottery after not even having the money to buy a lottery ticket!

Susan smiled. "Hey, come on in. It seems like you have had a stroke of luck. Tell me all the details."

Catherine walked in behind her and closed the door. "Well, it's not a lottery, but I guess fate is being generous." She could not stop smiling.

Susan bounced on the couch and flashed another smile. "Details?" she repeated, her eyes expressing eager curiosity.

"Ummm, not now. Let things work out first, and then it's a promise: you will be the first person I tell."

Susan looked a bit disappointed, but knowing the situations Catherine had been through, she did not push her.

"So what brings you here then?" she asked pleasantly.

"I wanted the hair dryer."

"Oooo! Did you finally hook up a millionaire?"

"No, babes. It's an interview tomorrow, and I need to look presentable."

"Where is it?" Susan was excited.

"Can't tell you," she said playfully.

"All right—as you say, *Your Highness*. But I want every detail after it."

Walking over to the worn-out cabinet beside the bed, Susan took out the hair dryer from the right drawer. Handing it over to Catherine, she teased, "This would be fifty bucks for a day."

Catherine grabbed the machine and, flashing a bright smile, replied, "When I get my first paycheck, I'll pay you fifty-five."

They laughed at the very idea.

Chapter 10: Amanda

His hand trailed down her side, along her waist, and further down.

He was lying flat on her, and that suffocated her.

Grabbing her hair, he pulled her neck closer and started sucking. He was pinching her and biting her neck.

There was no pleasure in it. It was only hurting.

She tried to scream, but could not. In desperation, she began pushing and kicking him off her.

She could not breathe.

She desperately needed air. She felt her lungs would burst.

Clutching at some invisible support, she jerked up, inhaling as much air as possible.

Amanda was drenched with perspiration. She was out of breath and completely disoriented.

Brad immediately took her in his arms and calmed her down.

She had evidently had a bad dream and was shivering uncontrollably.

Turning to him, she hugged him tightly and began sobbing. She did not want Brad to see her this way. She had to tell him what was bothering her.

Hugging her back, he promised that he would get her out of this torment soon.

Amanda did not know what to do, but she knew one thing: she had to stop torturing Brad.

Nestling deep in his arms, she found her peace.

And there she slipped into sleep, wishing she would never have dreams again.

Chapter 11: Catherine

Catherine's morning proved quite beautiful.

She slept two extra carefree hours. When she woke up, the sun blazed on her face, so she finally gave up the bed and lazily strolled to the kitchen.

Making a steaming cup of coffee, she switched on the television. As she surfed through the channels, her mind grew distracted. She was anxious about how her interview with the president would go.

She had ironed her clothes last night. She had also prepared a new copy of her résumé and qualifications documents. Now she could not wait for this time to pass before arriving at the president's office.

After her lavish breakfast of sausages and bread and another cup of coffee, Catherine took two extra minutes to brush her teeth perfectly. Stepping inside the hot shower, she imagined what a great Christmas it would be, and it was coming up soon!

A long hot soak eased some of her anxiety. By the time she stepped out, she was fresh and ready for a pleasantly challenging day. Moving around in a towel, she switched on the hair dryer and began blowing the loose curls that fell on her bare shoulders.

After twenty minutes, she was finally satisfied with the results. She combed back the hair on top to give a puff, which complemented the bouncy curls.

Turning to her clothing, she realized that her undergarments were completely worn out. *Who is going to see them anyway?* she decided, smiling to herself. She quickly put them on.

She marveled every moment of the new-clothes-wearing ritual. It was ecstasy. Catherine applied a fair amount of makeup and slipped into her shoes.

She was ready to go. It was still 2 p.m., and she could not wait to leave. She wanted to be there well before time, so she gave in and set out for the interview of her life…

Right after saying her prayers.

*   *   *

At half past two, Catherine entered the reception lounge of Immaculate University. After two visits, the place was starting to look hospitable. She could feel a connection with the surroundings.

Walking to the reception desk, she declared, "I have an appointment with the president."

The girl at the desk looked astonished.

Catherine realized she had been over-confident again, so she quickly amended, "I mean an appointment with Dr. Hopkins. I am Catherine Smith."

The receptionist searched through her list of appointments.

Catherine interjected, "Well, It was supposed to be at four, but I came early."

Catherine's informal attitude evidently annoyed the young lady. Her tone stiff, she informed her, "Please take a seat. You will be called in a while."

This was not a very positive start. Why did she not bite her tongue before such an awkward outburst? She quickly found a seat and took a deep breath.

Looking around, she noticed that the tall, suspicious-looking man was still at the entrance of the passage. When she settled down, he turned around and disappeared inside. She wondered what his name was. When her memory did not support her for another two minutes, she let it go and kept looking around.

The clock above the reception desk ticked slowly. Catherine was beginning to get tired. At one point, she had to stifle a yawn. The anxiety of the day was now settling, and she was feeling sleepy.

An hour passed like centuries.

By now, Catherine had shifted thrice on the couch, taken a tour of the whole lounge, and settled on a new spot directly opposite the passage leading to Dr. Hopkins's office.

Five minutes after Catherine had adjusted herself to her new location, the receptionist received a call. She conversed with the spy-guy, and he strode towards Catherine.

He spoke in a deep voice, which was even more sardonic than his personality. "Please follow me."

Not sure if she clearly understood what he said, she nevertheless felt encouraged by the change in the course of the afternoon's monotonous events. Grabbing at her papers she heaved up in an abnormal manner. The couch was too soft, and she had sunk deeply into it, so it was taking extra effort to get up. Holding the papers close to her chest, she applied all her pressure on the arm of the couch. Her legs spread out in opposite directions, and the first part of her body that rose was her unimpressive butt. When she finally stood straight, she grinned widely at the huge man waiting for her.

"Thank you, Mr. . . ."

"Sebastian," he reminded her, giving her a funny look.

He must wonder what the problem was with this lady. Yes, she was aware of the bizarre image she was presenting. All she could do was smile as if she had done something admirable.

Catherine had not yet balanced when Sebastian started walking towards Anthony's office. She leaped after him. Reaching the office, he paused, knocked very lightly, and opened the door. Peeking inside, he muttered something in his hollow voice, then stepped aside, leaving space for Catherine to enter.

Taking a deep breath, Catherine stepped into the familiar office.

When Sebastian closed the door, Anthony greeted her warmly. He looked her over and seemed pleased with how she looked. He had already made two cups of coffee for her initial briefing. "Relax a bit," he suggested, "before I take you to the president's office.

Catherine's heart went out for such hospitality. She could not believe there were still such good people. No matter how much she tried to look business-like, her grin would not disappear. Dr. Hopkins was a considerate gentleman who clearly showed his concern for her problems. They chatted for some time until his phone rang.

Reaching for it over the desk, he pleasantly greeted the caller, "Hello, Ms. Sinclair." He listened for a moment, then responded, "Yes, Ms. Smith is in my office, and I will be coming over with her. See you, ma'am."

Replacing the receiver, he waved at Catherine in a friendly manner. "Let's go, ma'am. The president is waiting for you."

Catherine followed Dr. Hopkins. Her stomach suddenly felt bubbly, and a strange taste simmered in her mouth. Swallowing it, she tried to ignore the chill she was feeling on her skin as she walked confidently behind the angel of a man.

The passage ended at a huge set of double doors with a nameplate in bold lettering: *President.* Opening the door on the right, Dr. Hopkins guided her into a large hall. Rather than carpeting, it had a shiny white marble floor with a huge desk placed opposite the door. The walls were spotless except for a painting of Abraham Lincoln hanging behind the desk.

Blossoming creepers decorated both corners. What a refreshing contrast to the dimly lit passage! The right corner featured a long window covered with beige blinds. To the left of the desk a door led to another room.

The name on the door read:

Matheus F. Gale, PhD
President

Catherine was impressed by everything here!

Dr. Anthony greeted the lady behind the desk. As she rose to greet him back, she had a tense smile, and she moved stiffly. The nameplate on her table read *Sinclair Adams*. She did not make eye contact with Catherine.

Dr. Hopkins inquired about the status of the interview. Told the president was available, he turned to Catherine and counseled, "You are at the right place. Now your efforts and capabilities will prove whether or not you deserve this job. All the best, ma'am." With that he left.

With a mechanical smile, Ms. Sinclair gestured to Catherine that she should proceed towards the office. Catherine knocked on the door and was invited in. The room she entered was again a contrast to the hall outside. It was heavily furnished. The furniture was made of ornate teak wood. The carpet was so soft and thick that Catherine had to steady herself. The desk was placed on the left wall from the entrance. On the right wall was a marvelous three-seater couch and a glass table. The wall opposite the entrance included a large window which was completely covered with solid wooden shutters. A huge TV monitor covered half the wall, but took the view of the whole room. Its shining concave screen displayed Catherine standing in the middle of the room.

Catherine couldn't hide her awe. Dr. Gale scrutinized her while she was absorbing her surroundings. Finally he asked her to take the seat opposite him. Glancing at her résumé, he announced, "How can you expect to get a job here with such an unimpressive résumé?"

This was a blow. Catherine was not prepared for this. She felt she had been struck by a truck.

She hadn't recovered fully from the initial shock when he spat, "What makes you think you can get an opportunity to be a part of my Immaculate University?"

The way he emphasized *my* showed how dear this university was to him. Feeling defeated under his scrutinizing gaze and hawkish face, Catherine went blank. Out of desperation, her tears started creeping down her cheeks. But his expressions did not change. Catherine wondered what was happening but had no clue.

She had completely surrendered, and this seemed to please him. Then he softened his expression a bit. She hung on his every gesture, his words, his expressions, and they all affected her. It felt like the flow of electricity to a bulb that he was controlling.

Walking to the left corner behind him, he poured sherry in a single glass and offered it to her.

She was stunned by this move. His authoritative gaze led her hand to hold the glass automatically. A sip of the tasty liquid eased her tense muscles.

Leaning by the desk, he looked at her for a few seconds and spoke in a much softer tone. "Unfortunate it is, that you did not finish your education. There are many qualified people available. What other work can you do?"

This was Catherine's turn to speak, but she did not know what to say.

He saw that. Patting her shoulder, he said, "Why don't you go back home to your family?"

Catherine knew this was impossible. Tears started rolling down again.

To sooth her, he smiled gently and said, "Don't worry, if you keep trying you will find a job."

Catherine's tears flowed faster.

To her surprise, he bent and hugged her shoulders tightly. "If you cannot find a job elsewhere, come back and talk to me."

Catherine did not know what to do. The situation she was worsening, she could not risk losing this opportunity. Dr. Hopkins's advice replayed in her mind: *Now your efforts and capabilities will prove whether or not you deserve this job.*

Catherine was still crying, so Dr. Gale held her closer…

And his hand brushed over her bosom.

She jumped and pulled away. It must have happened by accident. She collected herself.

To her surprise, the president's expression again became stern. He barked, "Well, if you are ready to look elsewhere, leave immediately."

He was so loud that Catherine got embarrassed about what the lady outside might think. Pondering all the options, Catherine gave up and bowed her head.

His voice softened, which raised her hope. "If you obey me, there will be work for you today."

When Catherine did not say anything, he proceeded. This time he touched her openly.

Catherine trembled, but did not resist.

After some time he said, "I knew you were a sensible girl." When he tried to intensify his actions Catherine hesitated.

Before she could respond, he pushed her away and shouted, "I was wrong about you. Just leave!" Then he walked back to his large seat behind the desk.

Catherine could not afford to lose this employment opportunity. She pleaded that she was sorry and would do just as he said.

This was the chance of a lifetime.

Chapter 12: Sinclair

Sinclair Adams felt sorry for the new girl. She had deliberately not made eye contact with her because she knew when she came out she would wish to be invisible.

She could hear the drama being staged inside. Gale was doing his horrendous tricks again, and the poor girl was falling for it. After the second time Gale yelled, Sinclair heard the girl sobbing loudly. She was obviously begging him, and she was pushing him away. In a matter of minutes, everything got the way it always does.

Sinclair wanted to block out the filth he was uttering while hitting the new girl. All this went on for twenty minutes. Then the new girl walked out clumsily. Dodging Sinclair's gaze, she quickly made her exit.

Sinclair wondered if she was photographed or videotaped.

* * *

Catherine had no choice. She did everything Matheus asked her.

When the so-called interview completed, Matheus looked at her triumphantly. "You can start your job tomorrow," he announced. "Welcome to Immaculate University."

Catherine dressed in silence and hurried out of the office, not daring to look back. Once she stepped out, Ms. Adams glanced at her, then returned to the papers on the desk.

On her way out, Catherine felt everyone was staring at her.

Practically running, she wildly waved at the bus. She climbed in and huddled in one corner.

When she reached home, Susan was waiting for her at the doorstep. Rushing past her she locked herself in her apartment.

She cried the whole evening until she slept.

Chapter 13: Brad

Brad stood there on the edge of the cliff, lost in the shifting shimmers of late-afternoon sun dappling the waters of Lake Tahoe. Thinking of Amanda, as he did every minute now, made him angry, then sad, then . . .

She had always wanted to travel and meet new people, although she hardly talked to strangers, and wanted to pursue her lifetime dream of writing. Her job had occupied her so much that she barely had time to do anything creative. He had wanted so very much to steal her away from Falcon Heights, to bring her to this paradise, to hold her and protect her, to show her such beauty in what could be an ugly world.

The images of the Monday morning sickened him. He had been trying to reach Amanda by phone, but she was not responding. He panicked and decided to pay her a visit.

When he walked into her apartment, he saw that she was lying in a pool of blood. She had cut her wrist, and now she wasn't moving, wasn't breathing.

He hugged her, but she slumped limply in his arms.

He felt a faint pulse.

A breath.

Carrying her in his arms, he rushed to the elevator. It was taking forever, so he found the stairway, carried her bodily, rushed down the lobby.

The watchman called for an ambulance, then assisted with first aid. They applied pressure to her wrist.

Brad held her tightly, pleading for her to live.

The watchman kept saying something about a man in an SUV who had disturbed her, but Brad was too preoccupied to pay attention.

The ride in the ambulance, rushing into the emergency room, the trauma team . . .

And the longest three hours of his life passed, and she regained consciousness!

He finally saw her breathing through the respirator and looking at him weakly, and he sighed with relief.

Today, standing with her at the edge of the cliff and looking at the heavenly view, he was glad she decided to quit her job. Hugging her tightly, he kissed her forehead. Amanda pressed closer to him and, smelling his neck, she struggled up and bit his chin!

The early Amanda was coming back. Her eyes had their sparkle back, and she was smiling again.

This is what he wanted.

This was the essence of their relationship: love, trust, and fun. And they would enjoy those again. Amanda would return to New York, and she would pursue her writing career, safe in the home they would make together.

Still, why did she not share the awful truth, such a big thing, with him? Only the watchman's comment tipped him off. Part of him was angry at her for keeping it to herself and slowly submitting. Since the night she confided in him, she had been even more stressed that he would leave her. He had been disappointed that she still did not know him. How could she consider him to be a shallow person who would leave her for doing something as a result of blackmail? He wished only that she had confided in him the same day. Matheus would have faced his punishment a month ago.

When Amanda finally told him from her hospital bed about what happened, she could not meet his eyes. She kept twitching her hands, which only hurt them by pulling against the IV tubes. She would stutter and run out of words, cringing at the memory of that cadaverous man assaulting her. She still had not told him exactly what happened in detail, but maybe he really did not want to know.

He knew enough.

And he would settle the score with Matheus F. Gale for ever laying hands on his Amanda.

Chapter 14: Matheus

Matheus F. Gale walked into the auditorium with his signature arrogance.

Today my Immaculate University will leave all the competitors behind.

With a capacity of more than two-thousand people, the place was packed. Cameras and a respectable press corps testified to the importance of this to Matheus's plans for the institution and its icon, the flashing star.

Matheus had been working indefatigably to ensure that his Immaculate University stood among the best in the United States, and his efforts were finally being recognized. A top-tier marketing company had arranged a conference on the future of higher education, during which the best universities would present their profiles. The conference participants included executives from major companies, senior government officials, and private professionals from every sphere to discuss partnerships, linkages, new program development, and international accreditation. University presidents and chancellors were ready to seize the moment

The conference had already started, and two universities had presented their profiles. Matheus laughed to himself at their efforts. He was the best, and he would prove it soon enough.

Next to him Anthony seemed anxious. Matheus smiled at this man's sincerity and dedication. The poor fellow was so stressed that he kept looking around like a mad man. Lightly squeezing his arm, Matheus told him to calm down, but it did not help.

When the presentation for Stanford University concluded, the chairman stepped back onto the podium. "And now I would like to call upon the president of Immaculate University," he announced in the same tone he had used for all the previous universities.

Matheus got pretty much offended by it, but brushed it aside. He was already annoyed by Anthony's distracting gestures. It was not the host's fault, but rather Anthony's for making him uncomfortable.

He stood up slowly and gracefully. He could feel every single eye on him as the spotlight followed him slowly. He approached the foot of the stairs leading to the stage, then paused for a couple of seconds. When he started hearing restless murmurs from the crowd, he smiled inwardly and looked up at the logo of *his* Immaculate University. The bright star still glistened in the semi-dark hall.

He sensed many gazes from the audience also following his. His dramatic pause complete, Matheus moved up the stairs and rapidly strode towards the podium.

Here, where several unimpressive leaders had tried selling their substandard universities' mediocre programs, Matheus F. Gale stood broadly and with flair. He was deliberately taking his time because this was his moment. He had to prove that the great university he nurtured was running the best among all contesting.

Basking in the glow of the spotlight, he surveyed the waiting crowd. Ahead of him the dimly lit auditorium showed a sea of myriad expressions: expectation, impatience, confusion, and even boredom. Matheus knew he would merge all of these varying emotions into one: *appreciation.*

"Success is our destination!" he announced, pausing for emphasis. "We at Immaculate University believe in nothing but perfection. Our highly professional and accredited programs have served many of our students—students who are now working at many of the most highly respected and renowned institutions across the US and around the world. *My* Immaculate University is home of world's best professionals."

Once he had started, he knew no one could stop him. He was proud that he had this forum to present his beloved possession to such influential audiences.

After a little pause, he continued with renewed vigor. "This has not been a smooth journey. Never in this enduring voyage did I feel discouraged or drained. I kept my focus firm and my spirits high. Hard work is always repaid—and repaid immensely. My Immaculate University is achieving every milestone I envisioned. It has been a long and indefatigable struggle. Many who joined hands with me have given up under the enormous effort required to produce such great results, but I was never defeated."

Lowering his head, he closed his eyes and visualized the scenario when Immaculate University would earn the award for outstanding achievement by an institution of higher learning, which would happen in just a few minutes.

When he opened his eyes and gazed around, every person was anxiously waiting for him to continue. This was absolute power. He was controlling every pulse in the huge hall. With his signature smirk he proudly announced, "Now I present how we have struggled to achieve the stature of pre-eminent university." He waved his arm dramatically towards the large screen behind him, which lit immediately as if under his command. The bright star began its travels, illuminating every passage until it finally halted at top, brightening those two exquisite words:

Immaculate University.

Matheus smiled brightly and watched the audience's faces. Everyone was looking at the screen intently. Their expressions shifted from amazement to shock and finally to disbelief. Matheus felt even more influential. He had captivated the crowd. He *owned* these people.

Then someone shouted, "What the hell is going on?"

Perplexed, Matheus turned to look at the screen and froze.

The screen blazed with image of a large desk, lying atop it a nude young woman in tears as a man stroked and slapped her, hissing orders for her to obey.

And the camera caught his face, a familiar face, the face of one esteemed university president:

Matheus F. Gale.

*   *   *

The young gentleman sitting next to Anthony pulled a thick manila envelope from inside his jacket and handed it to him. Smiling, he said, "This is surely much better than any annual increment."

Anthony took the envelope and thanked him with a broad smile.

The gentleman walked out of the hall and dialed a number. After two rings, it answered.

"Hey, James," the other end of the call said. "How did it go?"

"Mission accomplished, bro. Where should we meet to celebrate?"

"I'm at Graff. I'm sure Amanda won't go for any other diamond."

Brad knew today would be the best day to propose to her.

F A T E

FATE

They say that fate is like being raped,

You can't fight it, so just learn to enjoy it.

This statement has been circulated mainly to bring smiles to faces, but just once, read it seriously.

To tell you the truth, it gives me goose bumps! It brings out a major reality that no matter how much we plan and attempt to execute it, there is always a ceiling above. Past it, everyone is powerless.

Is it good or bad?

That remains the question.

Mother Nature returns to us what we give Her. Give good and you will get outstanding, but if you go around spreading negativity, you will certainly be getting very bad news. So do analyze what you are doing and foresee the consequences of how it could backfire. Anything that we do is automatically inspected by the larger circle called nature; and when the right time comes, we are compensated for all our doings. No wonder it is said:

What goes around, comes around!

What do you think Matheus deserves after considering himself some supreme power? He thought nothing could beat him. His belief was to buy whatever came along. But what he never realized was that there are other buyers in the market too—buyers so influential that they could even dictate his pawns. Alas, only if man had enough foresight. God has blessed everyone with intelligence, but how we utilize it defines our wisdom.

Luck is truly only chance. Not everyone could be lucky. Surely there could have been many instances when Matheus must have been in hot water, but not learning from his previous experiences was utterly his mistake.

Would you like to know what happened to him afterwards?

You do! All right, I won't make you wait anymore.

Let "Hunter Hunted" tell you the story.

HUNTER HUNTED

Chapter 15: Matheus

The screen was showing his *private* videos!—images of him training his employees to be obedient and submissive!

The girl he hired a month ago was climaxing as he slapped her around—a fake orgasm, he could see now.

Panicking, he yelled, "Stop the projector," but the screen transformed into another scene on the couch: Matheus pulling another of his employees on top, then jerking her up and down until she climaxed.

The crowd was on its feet, some shouting, angrily demanding explanation. He tried to find a power cord to pull, but the light blinded him, the images shocking even him.

Another scene started, and he joined the chorus demanding that this be stopped. He did not know how to escape this hell. For the first time, he felt helpless. He wanted to escape, so he headed for the stairs, but two uniformed officers blocked his way.

His legs felt like jelly. This was *not* what he planned. He was trapped.

The officers grabbed his arms and turned him around, then handcuffed him and escorted him to the backstage area. They said something about his rights, suggested he not say anything, then led him down a passageway and out of the building. People were coming out the main doors to watch, casting gazes of disgust and contempt at him. He felt as he were suffocating. The open air did not help. Everyone was talking about him, in the worst manner. One man spit on the ground at Matheus's feet.

The officers ushered him into a Jeep and sped him somewhere he did not want to go. His brain stopped supporting his senses. He could not think of anyone to call for help. Desperately he fished in his pockets for his phone and discovered that it had already been confiscated.

This was ungodly horrible!

The nightmare worsened when the Jeep stopped and they pushed his head down so he could not see. He was callously guided inside a smallish building, maybe a police station, to a small holding cell with a stainless-steel table bolted to a concrete floor and a mirror along one wall, obviously a one-way glass.

They pushed him in and locked the door of steel bars, leaving him on display. He could hear people talking about him in another room, the door ajar.

After a horrendously long wait, three uniformed guards entered the cubicle and ordered him to undress. He protested, but they were unmoved. When he did not oblige their orders, to his utter shock they grabbed him and shocked him with a Taser!

He lay on the concrete floor, twitching, his arms and legs contorted, every part of his body beyond his control. It hurt like nothing had ever hurt before. The bright lights seemed to flash and pulse, his eyes unable to focus. Drool leaked from the side of his mouth and ran down his cheek. For a man who carried himself with a certain level of class and style, this was humiliating.

The officers stood over him and watched, chuckling, remarking to each other about the "esteemed" president not looking so esteemed right now.

"Maybe he needs to be slapped to his senses," one remarked, "like he does helpless women."

Then they fell upon him, handling him roughly, alternately restraining him limbs while they forcibly stripped him. His diamond cuff links scattered across the bare floor. In barely a minute he sprawled stark naked. Then they grabbed his arms and legs and roughly lifted him to the cold steel table.

The two biggest overpowering hulks pinned him down while the third officer grinned lasciviously, then ceremoniously donned a pair of purple rubber gloves, smartly snapping each one at the wrist.

"I think this one might be harboring some contraband," one of the pinning hulks announced, eliciting chuckles from the others.

"Let's have a look, shall we?" suggested the gloved one, who then proceeded to start inspecting Matheus all over.

His hands went through Matheus's hair, feeling every part of his skull. Moving down his neck, he pressed at every nerve. Then he forcefully opened his mouth and ordered the helpless man to stick out his tongue, lift it, and move it side to side.

Matheus had enough. He tried to break free, but was pushed down hard against the cold table, which sent chills all over him. Then the gloved cop moved down toward his groin. The other hulks helped him spread Matheus's legs so he could grope him, all the while displaying a crooked smile.

None of them moved.

One of the officers taunted, "So that's the offending instrument he's been using to have so much fun all this time."

"At innocent women's expense," another added.

"Not so impressive, is it?" taunted the third.

They all laughed.

Matheus tried to struggle again, but they slapped him, then seemed to find that ironically amusing. So he gave up and closed his eyes tightly and waited for the nightmare to end.

Then it got worse.

He caught a whiff of petroleum scent, then felt something cold between his cheeks as a hand grabbed his thigh and a slippery finger slid painfully inside his anus.

He squawked.

Clearly not a trained physician, the man seemed intent on making it hurt, and he succeeded.

Matheus grunted pitifully, ashamed of both what was happening and his own weakness.

The hand continued to dig in, and Matheus's shouts grew louder with every jerk. The torture went on and on.

By the time the officer released his hand Matheus was too exhausted even to move. He lay there, panting and squirming, unable to relieve the excruciating pain.

None of them showed any mercy. Rather, they kept grinning and glancing at each other, both as if to egg each other on and congratulate themselves for what they had done.

Matheus twisted and turned on the table as the pain spread all over in ascending waves, starting from his belly and rolling up to his skull. Finally, the horrid sensations gradually diminished, transforming into heat that spread out to his limbs. His body burning, the freezing table sent electrifying shocks that extended the waves of pain.

One of the officers said, "We should let him gather himself for the moment. After all, that tight hole could very well be a pleasant surprise for us tonight." Looking into Matheus's eyes, he made a ring of the index finger and thumb of his left hand, then slid the middle finger of his right hand in and out the hole.

Amused by the horrified look on Matheus's face, they roared with laughter and high-fived each other before they left.

Alone again in the cubicle, this time undressed and feeling even more vulnerable, Matheus trembled in fear of what might be coming next. He couldn't bear being touched again in such a disgusting manner. He could not stand the idea of being forced to be the object of anyone's twisted sexual pleasure. At that moment, he felt what all those young girls must have felt when he trained them for submission.

Hours passed and nothing happened. Matheus had pulled himself together and slid off the table. When he looked around for his clothes he could not find anything. The air-conditioning had been turned up so high Matheus was freezing. To protect himself he crouched in a corner and began rubbing his hands together and over other shivering parts of body. His mind was now running through all the probabilities of who had plotted this against him, who had been the traitor, what would happen next, how many of the men outside would feast on him, how painful it would be, and it went on. The whole scenario of the seminar played over and over in his mind. Nothing unusual struck him. All his trusted pawns had been there, and none of them had the audacity of even breathing without his permission. He could not think of who could have let out the secret. He could see his naked self in the mirror opposite him. He knew he was being watched, and he did not want to give them any more evidence.

Chapter 16: Sergeant Dave

Behind the one-way mirror Sergeant Dave Hyde observed Matheus closely.

He had been watching the whole scene since he was brought in. What was going on in this man's mind? He was huddled in a corner, but his expressions were very calculated. *How could he sleep peacefully at night?* Sergeant Hyde had been practicing without success, trying to sleep through even one night by burying painful memories.

This day had started slowly, and the sergeant was hoping to leave early. Then Officer Aaron ordered snacks and asked him to stay for a while to hang out with the young fellows. He had agreed even though his wife, Diana, would be waiting with dinner and would be upset if he came late. Dave was fond of this young man so he agreed to stay back. He could not say no to him when he urged staying for a cup of coffee and a final game of Bridge. The game was in full swing when the office phone rang and nobody was willing to move. Therefore, Dave allowed the chaps to enjoy the game and took his tuna sandwich into his office.

"Sergeant Dave Hyde," he said authoritatively. Victor was on the other end. The impatience in his tone disturbed Dave, and the words Victor spoke killed Dave's appetite. Placing the sandwich in his napkin, he listened to Victor in silence. When he finished explaining the whole case, Dave ordered, "Bring him in!" and slammed the phone.

Dave knew Victor hated having to call him about such a case. This would stir up Dave's turmoil again. It had taken a lot of time and effort to find even brief moments of peace with the tragedy of his daughter. Hearing what this Matheus Gale fellow had done sent images of Agnes flashing through Dave's mind.

Agnes had been excited about her sixteenth birthday. One day before the big day she had planned a day of shopping with her friends. He felt that hurried peck she dropped on his cheek with the most beautiful smile he had ever seen. Diana had instructed them to be careful and be back before sunset, but they wanted to dine out, and her Barbie-doll expression had pushed him to agree. She and her friends had all been excited, and he could never say no to his little doll. The moment he said yes, all the girls squealed with joy. Then all the girls floated out.

Two seconds later, Agnes popped her head in and brightened his evening with, "I love you, Dad. You're the best."

That was the last time he saw her smile.

Agnes did not return.

Frantic, he and Diana started calling around, looking for her.

Then came the phone call. Victor was the one who informed him a body had been found. The most difficult day of his life had ended with holding his wife while they identified the body of their little girl, the victim of rape and murder. It was his own baby, whom he had always protected like a delicate flower. He could barely look at her bruised face before Victor escorted them out of the morgue.

Instead of celebrating her birthday, Agnes's devastated parents rested her in peace.

Now Sergeant Dave Hyde stood here looking at this animal crouched in a corner. He wanted to barge in and stab him until he died. The pain of losing a daughter was excruciating, and the realization that her uncaught killer was someone similar to this beast ignited him.

Victor stood next to him, saying something, but Dave could not concentrate. He turned to Victor and quietly said, "Let's move slowly here. I want to delay his making any contact to ask for help."

He left the room. Chapter 17: Matheus

Matheus wondered what would happen next. The officers had expressed their intentions, and as the night passed, his insecurity grew. Every time he sensed movement nearby, he jumped. Other times, exhaustion crept in, and he could hardly keep his eyes open. He had spent sleepless nights to put on an outstanding show at the seminar, and this was the last place he could have thought of ending up.

Sometime in the middle of the night, the door clicked open and one of the bulky officers entered—holding a metal rod.

Matheus recalled his threatening gesture. This was not good.

Already shivering with extreme cold, he trembled even more. This was really bad news. Matheus shrank into his corner.

The officer had a livid look on his face. His eyes were swollen and red, and he was fuming. He grabbed Matheus by the shirt and pulled him to his feet, then clenched his fist and punched him hard in his face, crashing him on the floor.

For a moment Matheus could not comprehend what had happened. He felt that his jaw had probably dislocated, but he was too numb and terrified to protest. Before he could gather himself, the officer grabbed his hair and pulled him. Fixing his knee on Matheus's back he pressed his entire weight. Matheus wailed with excruciating pain. Desperately he groped for anything to hold on to, but found nothing.

The officer yelled, "What did you think? You would escape after ruining all those people's lives?" He pulled Matheus's hair farther, choking him. Punching his shoulder, the officer continued even louder. "Now I'll show you what happens when you get caught. First, you get your ass kicked—" Another punch! "Then you hit the wall!" Pulling him up, he slammed Matheus against the wall twice. "Then you get the same pleasure you gave all those girls—with intensity."

This was the worst part.

The cop pushed his face into the floor and tugged at his clothes. He squirmed but couldn't get away. He tried to cry out, but the brute pressed down on his neck, taking his breath.

And he felt it.

Something hard. A rod.

It was entering his anus, being shoved. Harder. Farther.

The pain was unbearable. Matheus jerked hard, got his head turned, and he shouted with anguish.

Another officer barged in and grabbed the bulky officer. "What the hell are you up to? Aaron, you're gonna kill him."

He pulled him back, but Aaron did not budge.

And Matheus knew this was it. He was about to die.

Two other officers rushed in and pulled at Aaron. After a long struggle, they dragged him out and locked Matheus back in isolation. The weapon disappeared. Matheus tugged his clothing back into place and curled into the fetal position on the floor.

Tears filled his eyes, and he had trouble catching his breath.

The chilled emptiness of the room felt better than anything he could imagine. He tried not to imagine what would have happened if the others had not come in.

But imagine, he did.

*   *   *

"Control yourself, Aaron," arresting officer Victor demanded. Pushing him into a chair, he shouted, "I didn't tell you everything for you to get emotional. It's fool behavior like that'll bring the feds in here investigating *civil rights violations.*

As Aaron started to calm down, Victor handed him a glass of water, which he pushed away. "Look, we deal with crime, and crime has many faces. We need to have—"

"Leave me alone," Aaron growled, cutting him off mid-sentence. Victor realized he had no other option, so he quietly left.

This situation was getting out of control.

*   *   *

Left alone in the room, Aaron felt helpless. His heart went out for Sergeant Dave, who had been so composed and helpful even after going through such turmoil in his life only eight months ago. Aaron had joined this station two months after that accident, and Sergeant Dave had been nothing but protective, helpful, and encouraging. He wanted everyone to appreciate and be proud of their job.

Many evenings Sarge had pushed everyone to crash his home unannounced, then urged them to linger until his generous wife would serve them with her special country-recipe pepper steaks and lasagna. They would sit in the courtyard and smoke until late at night, by which time Aaron would be cracking nonsense jokes and imitating everyone. Dave always laughed with them and treated them all like his own children. Aaron wanted to salute him for such character and strength. He wanted to do anything possible to make him happy.

This man deserved the utmost respect.

Victor stuck his head in the room. "Go on, Aaron. Take a break."

Aaron didn't want to take a break; he wanted to break something, to break some*body*.

He sighed and rubbed his face. Victor wouldn't go away until Aaron was gone, so the big man stood, nodded, and headed for the vending machines.

Chapter 18: Sergeant Dave

As he headed toward home, Sergeant Dave Hyde longed to be with Diana, the woman who had stood by him even as he had stood by her through the whole turmoil. She was completely alone for long stretches after Agnes, but she never tried to make him feel guilty about it.

When he stepped inside the house, Diana was in the kitchen. The click of the door alerted her, and she entered the hallway with a smile to greet Dave. Her smile died the moment she saw Dave's expression.

"Have they found who hurt our little girl?" she wondered.

He shook his head.

She embraced him.

Dave let loose all the stress and hugged her. They stood in each other's shelter for a long time.

When Diana finally moved, Dave hugged her tighter. He had fallen in love with this woman twenty years ago when she first hugged him, and she could charm him still. He had never hidden how he relied on her. He knew she was aware that sometimes he deliberately showed dependence to make her feel secure, but today he couldn't hide that something had shaken him.

He was not in a good shape.

Diana gave him all the space and time he needed. He only wanted silence, and she provided it.

Dave had no idea how long he stood in the hallway. Finally, he let her loose and slipped his arm around her waist, then walked her towards the living room.

When they settled on the couch, Diana kissed him lightly. Resting her head on his shoulder she rubbed his chin and asked, "What's bothering you, sweetheart?"

Dave had known Diana not just as a partner, but as a best friend for a very long time. He knew that he would only feel better if he shared this with her. "A man was brought to the station today." He fell silent again.

Diana was patient.

"He raped young women and photographed them. Then he made them work in his university and molested them regularly."

Diana's reaction seemed hurt more than shocked.

He wondered what she was thinking. "He is the president of a university."

Diana's blank expression annoyed him. He could not understand how sometimes she could hide all her feelings behind this beautiful face. He wanted her to react the way he had. He wanted to hear how this news had brought the flood of Agnes's memories back. He did not want pity on his helplessness; rather, he wanted the same anger and humiliation.

Out of frustration he grabbed her shoulders and spoke between gritted teeth. "Say something. Say that you miss Agnes, too. Say that this bizarre news has reminded you of what happened to our Agnes, our angel, our life."

Diana stiffened against his grip, but tears streamed down her crimson cheeks. "Dave, don't do this," she managed after a struggle. She was shaking.

Dave hugged her and she cried. Both of them cried for a long time until they could not anymore. Somewhere in those sobs, embraces, and painful memories, Diana fell asleep. Settling her head on the cushion, he wrapped her in a blanket and walked into Agnes's room.

He was welcomed by a framed portrait of Agnes on the wall.

She had flashed her brightest smile when he took that picture. He flinched at the pain he felt deep inside. There was not a day when he did not think about her, and today he missed her more than ever.

Sitting at her study, he lifted the small picture frame containing their lovely family photo. He remembered the day when he had pressured both Diana and Agnes to dress up formally and go to the studio to pose for this. Agnes had been furious. She worried that her friends would make fun of her. Her constipated expression made him smile.

Holding the frame close to his chest, he dozed off, promising himself that Matheus would face the worst fate he could imagine.

Chapter 19: Aaron

Dawn brought more bad news for Matheus.

An anonymous manila envelope was delivered to the police station. Aaron had slept uncomfortably on the chair, twisting and turning. When Derek tapped his shoulder, he jerked awake. He had experienced several crazy dreams throughout the night. The unannounced tap ticked him off.

Snatching the package from Derek's hand, he slammed it on the desk. He needed to hit the can before starting a crazy new day. After taking his time in the restroom, he resumed his place and examined the package. It provided no clue as to where it came from, and Aaron wasn't feeling any particular curiosity when he tore it open to check its contents.

To his utter shock, it supplied visual evidence of everything he had imagined about Matheus the night before. There was a stack of pictures displaying the pervert committing his crimes against several defenseless girls. He donned rubber gloves and started filling out an evidence check-in log to preserve the chain. As he sifted through them, flipping from one to the another, his temper flared continuously. His hands were visibly shaking as he applied numbered stickers to the back of each photo.

He also found a couple of CDs, and Aaron had a good idea what they contained. The more he looked at the pictures, the more he was convinced he deserved the pleasure of killing the animal trapped in his custody.

Victor sensed trouble when he walked in and saw Aaron's glaring eyes.

Aaron responded to the unspoken question by scattering pictures across the desk.

Gathering them, Victor ordered, "After you tag 'em, bag 'em. Don't do anything else. Dave will be arriving soon, and he will decide what to do next."

Aaron did not like being a junior and, at this particular moment, he wished he were in charge. But he did realize that Victor was right. Containing his emotions, he remained quiet, but he did show his disapproval with a disappointed look.

Victor could not help but smile. Patting Aaron's shoulder, he told him to go home and take rest.

As usual, Aaron rejected the idea.

"Well, at least eat something, or you'll faint again. And trust me, you are too heavy to be lifted around." He was teasing Aaron about the funny evening when he had passed out after drinking too much.

Aaron couldn't help but smile. He did not remember much of what happened that night, but it definitely gave all the others his weak spot.

When Sergeant Dave arrived, everyone stood up. Aaron felt a sudden sense of protection. He was entranced by the aura of this gentleman. No one could deny his authority, but he himself carried himself with such grace that no one could feel intimidated in his presence. Waving everyone to relax, he strode towards Victor.

"Anything further on Matheus?"

"We received a packet of evidence. It's hard to look at, but it's damning." Handing the pictures to Dave, Victor followed the sergeant inside his office. Aaron proceeded, too, but Dave signaled him to wait, so he listened nonchalantly from near the doorway.

When Dave closed the door, Victor informed him that he had contacted Headquarters about the case and Detective Warren Fox from the Sex Crimes Unit (SCU) was on his way.

"He's the best man," Dave said, "to handle Matheus."

Derek announced that Warren had arrived.

Dave came out to greet him.

A portly man with perpetually arched eyebrows that could either register surprise or glare disapprovingly without much apparent effort, Warren smiled broadly and offered his meaty chuckle. "What have I heard, Davy? That you've kept a pervert in your custody?"

His stained teeth were just as filthy as Aaron remembered.

"*I'll* take custody," Warren said slyly. "It's been so long I had some fun." He flexed his wrists, openly showing his excitement. Dave always seemed to enjoy having Warren stop by the precinct. Nothing about them complemented each other, but they got along very well.

"Stay for a cup of coffee before the fun," Dave said. Exaggerating a peek behind him, he added, "I see you don't have your entourage with you today."

"Yeah, I left all those lazy bastards at home. Told 'em to get the, um, *interrogation* gear prepared for our new guest." He turned to Aaron. "So what's on the menu, fat boy?"

Aaron liked Warren, so he did not mind his comments. He stuffed his hands in his pockets and pulled them out, showing empty pockets, then pouted his lips like a baby.

Warren roared with laughter, shaking the walls. "Davy, I see you're starving your boys. Look how anorexic he is!" Beckoning Aaron, he said, "Let's feast on Fat Burger today. Order mine with extra cheese and a large Coke." Patting his bulging belly he turned to Dave. "Dude, I'm sure this would suit you, too. Having a goddamn flat gut at your age is not healthy."

Dave shook his head and asked Aaron to order breakfast. Aaron called in the order, then stood in the background and watched the men go through the stack of photos.

"This man is sure to have a piece of me. I'll hand this son-of-a-bitch to Viper. He loves fucking men. Let him have some fun, too. He's been with us for a long while. Maybe he deserves a treat." Noticing that Dave looked lost, he gently patted his shoulder and quietly said, "Let go of it. Past is only to be scanned for good memories." Dave nodded in agreement.

The burgers and Cokes arrived, so everyone took a break to eat. Finishing, Warren burped loudly and said, "I should be moving now. Hand that bastard over to me and I'll leave."

When they entered the cell, Matheus was sleeping, curled in one corner of the room, naked.

The sight amused Warren. Kicking Matheus's butt he shouted, "Get your naked ass moving. You're going to the big house."

Matheus sprang awake, looking like he was about to have a heart attack. Aaron moved menacingly closer, making the scared man cower in the corner.

Throwing the pair of trousers and shirt at Matheus, Warren ordered, "Wear this and get the hell up. I ain't got no time to see your little sausage shaking." Giving a final kick Warren left.

Aaron remained to stand watch while Matheus tried to dress, hands shaking, his body no doubt trembling from the cold. Matheus did manage to get his clothes on and step out into the warm room where he quickly noticed every eye on him.

The huge policeman at the exit barked, "If you're done sunbathing," Warren barked, "maybe now we can get moving, my fair lady?"

Derek turned Matheus around and cuffed him. Then with Aaron right behind him, Matheus quickly limped towards the exit, carefully avoiding Warren's penetrating gaze.

Climbing into the Jeep, Warren patted Harry, almost shaking him, and said loudly, "Let's move, my boy, the *balls* are in our court now." The emphasis on balls made Harry and Aaron smile.

As the Jeep zoomed away, Aaron stood there and watched. Finally he took a deep breath.

Then for the first time in hours, he unclenched his fists.

Chapter 20: Lt. Leonard

Lieutenant Leonard had been ready with all the arrangements as instructed by Detective Warren Fox. By now he was impatient, wondering why they had not arrived. It had been three hours for a drive of ninety minutes—max.

Still, with Warren this was not entirely unexpected. Having investigated countless criminal cases, neither had ever seen one like this. Rapists and molesters always had a distinct pattern in their history, and this was not new. Matheus had come from a family of eleven where brothers fought for bread. His early years were spent in the streets of Jacksonville. It started with being the delivery boy of the *special package* for the thugs of their area. They would slap him with his daily wages and insult him for his clumsy gestures. He seized a break when he smashed a bottle of cheap beer on K9's head one night while he was feasting on his tightness as usual. He fled Florida and never returned. Never shying away from hard work he did succeed in making an empire but what couldn't seize to surprise was; how could a smart person commit such foolish acts?

The contrast between the increasingly well-regarded university and having a forced brothel right in its own president's office was unbelievable. It was like setting all the pawns and bishops to checkmate the opponent's king, and in your final move bringing your own king in front of their queen. Leonard was still pondering this matter when his phone rang. "Lieutenant Leonard," he said authoritatively.

"Lieutenant, Detective Warren Fox has arrived," Jonas informed from the guard room.

"I'll be down to receive him." Replacing the receiver, he stretched his legs under the desk. "Okay, Mr. Matheus, let's meet!" This was interesting, and Leonard looked forward to it.

When Leonard arrived at the interrogation room, Warren was already seated there, involved in an intense discussion with Captain William over some pictures scattered on the table. He did not need to inquire about the topic because the pictures told the whole story.

"Nobody has tried to contact him, and he still hasn't asked for an attorney. He doesn't know we executed a search warrant and recovered the equipment he used, or that we already had these photos, which is enough evidence to keep him in Category A." Warren was saying.

He handed the pictures to Leonard when he approached, shifting his attention mid-sentence to invite his comments.

After taking a careful look at the pictures, Leonard gave his decision: "Get him in the uniform; Viper is waiting for him."

The moment the orders were passed, two guards shoved Matheus into the scanning room.

Warren's amusement was absolute.

Chapter 21: Matheus

Once again Matheus was stripped and inspected, inside and out. This time what disturbed him more was the fact that they did not bother to use any lubricant.

When they were done with inspection, they left a neatly folded fluorescent-orange uniform for him to wear. Matheus slipped into his new clothes and knocked on the door. The guard unlocked the door and guided him through a passage to meet the same detective accompanied by two others.

They discussed him right there as if he were not even present, a conversation revolving around him, full of mockery and name-calling. Matheus felt the most degraded at that moment. He realized that being stripped and spanked was only a physical torture, but being the target of humiliation through words bruised the soul. He could not interject, as every word they said was more or less true.

He wished he could disappear.

After a lengthy discussion, one of the officers said, "What the hell is he still doing here? Lock him up with Viper."

The disgust in his tone infuriated Matheus. Before he could react, he was pushed towards the dimly lit passage at the far end. The sight of the passage choked him. The distasteful fluid secreted between his teeth and his stomach churned. His heart started beating faster. Something did not feel good about that place. He wanted to resist, but did not have the energy.

The passage was blocked with a metallic gate. The guard swiped the access card and it slid open. Air inside was damp and smelled of chlorine. They moved swiftly towards the end. Matheus noticed that none of the cells they passed were occupied. A sudden sense of satisfaction swept over him. At least he would have some time in peace to plan ahead.

Right then he realized he had never even demanded a lawyer. Controlling his emotions, he told himself that he needed to strategize his next move. He would surely demand a lawyer soon. A self-contented smile twitched his lip as they reached the end of the passage. The guard in front unlocked the last cell and moved aside. Giving a thankful smile, Matheus proceeded inside, but stopped in mid-step. The tiny cell was already occupied by three inmates who seemed to be more than settled in.

Matheus's pause was neither welcomed nor appreciated, so the guard pushed him inside and locked the cell again without a word.

Matheus was perplexed. He needed space to sit down and plan, but here he had to adjust with three smelly people who, he was sure, had not seen school ever. This was nonsense but somehow it reminded him of his early days. Standing with his usual arrogance, he surveyed the tiny compartment. It contained two bunkbeds, one against each wall on the side, and a stainless-steel toilet with sink console was fixed on the wall opposite the entrance.

Two young guys who looked like mere teens sat on one of the beds and looked at him expectantly. Matheus shot them a look like, *I don't even like looking at you, so don't expect to converse with me.*

The other bed was occupied by the third inmate. He seemed to be sleeping.

Ignoring him, Matheus turned to the other two and spoke authoritatively. "Move out of this bed and clean it for me." He signaled at the pile of sheets at the foot of the bed. The others looked at him in silence. Matheus got annoyed at their lack of response, so he repeated, "Move!"

Behind him the other bed creaked. The other inmate was probably awake. Matheus deliberately ignored the sounds and concentrated on the two in front of him, both of whom seemed to be intimidated by him. After a few seconds, he felt that the third one was standing quite close to him. When he turned to see his third roommate, he stopped midway and gasped out loud. He could not believe what he saw.

This person was almost six-foot five, with a huge muscular body. His bare chest displayed a very daunting tattoo of a snake fighting a scorpion, the viper's tongue slit just below his left nipple. He had seen this image at the same proximity, years ago. The only difference was that that night he could escape but not today.

Matheus knew he was in danger. K9 scratched the head of the viper on his chest and looked down at Matheus. When he opened his mouth, Matheus heard hollow sounds, which were impossible to comprehend as words. He strained his ears to give it a try, but the response was a deafening roar.

Shivers waved throughout his body.

Then K9 lowered his head to look Matheus in the eyes and said in a thick accent, "Only I order in here, Matty. Keep that in mind, only *Viper* orders!" He surveyed the numb Matheus head to toe and slowly stuck out his tongue. Matheus was astonished to see that his tongue was also slit like the viper on his chest.

Then Viper signaled to the other two, who were evidently enjoying the scene and ordered, "Get him ready. I have some scores to settle."

Right at that instant they sprang to their feet and grabbed Matheus. To his utter shock they stripped him naked and pushed him to the floor, then tried to bend him over one of the bottom bunks. When he resisted, he was kicked and punched. When he finally gave up, they got him to bend over the bed.

One turned off the overhead cell light.

The other informed Viper, "He is ready."

Viper slowly got up and stretched. Cracking his knuckles, he approached Matheus and slowly ran his fingers along his back. When he reached his butt crack, he slid his fingers between the cheeks. Then he stopped and growled, "What's that?" Turning to the others he said, "Hand me the light."

Matheus was already humiliated, and he did not want to be raped in open light. He wished it all got over with in the dark. He was praying when he suddenly felt his skin burning.

He squirmed to escape and tried to cry out, but the two young guys held him down and one clamped a hand over Matheus's mouth.

Viper was instilling pain to get pleasure. He tried to shout his agony, but could not do anything. His hands were tightly gripped by the other two and his torso was held firm in Viper's hands.

He was still not over the pain of burning when Viper entered him. Matheus could feel that Viper was bigger than anything he had experienced since last night. He bellowed with pain, and one of the younger ones clamped his mouth harder with one hand.

Viper enjoyed Matheus for a long time, thrusting hard and deep, finally releasing all over Matheus's back.

After the whole session, Viper slumped back on his bed and quickly fell asleep.

The others let go and left Matheus on his own, and went back to their own business.

Matheus sprawled on the floor, bleeding.

One of the guys threw a small towel towards him and said, "Use it or you'll soak the floor with your blood. It's good for you because you'll be sleeping here the whole week."

Both of them laughed at Matheus.

*   *   *

As the week passed, Matheus experienced things from bad to worse. The only people he saw other than Viper and his two stooges was the guard who brought in food thrice a day and when an inmate with a cart took the dishes back. Matheus wanted to speak to some officer, but was too afraid of Viper's reaction. He wanted to call for his lawyer. He decided Anthony must be going around trying to get him out of this hell. That relieved his fears some, and gave him a bit of confidence. Yes, Anthony was working on this. He wondered only when it would be done.

One morning Matheus was lying on the floor, trying to adjust to any position that did not ache his body. The guard came over and said, "Gale! Matheus Gale! Come out; you've got visitors."

Matheus's heart raced. *Finally!* He was going to break free.

He practically crawled to the gate and waited like a dog about to be set free. When he stepped out in the dingy passage, the smell of chlorine even felt amazing. He walked close behind the guard so no one would be able to pull him back.

They passed some passages and electronic gates, then entered a room with a row of seats in front of windows, black telephone receivers on the wall next to each booth.

The guard indicated seat number 13 and told him to meet his visitor there.

Walking towards it, Matheus wondered what news this number 13 brought for him.

Then he stopped when he saw her. This visit would be as unlucky as the number 13. Seated on the other side of the window waited his wife, Nancy. She looked calm on the surface, but her glaring eyes told a different story. He wondered how many plates and wine glasses she had broken after getting drunk with frustration. Nancy's anger had always been uncontrollable. It had taken her a week to compose herself and meet him. Now it was his turn to face her wrath.

When he picked up the receiver Nancy did not bother to greet him. "I have filed for divorce and demanded fifty-million dollars plus expenses and attorney fees."

Matheus started to speak, but had nothing to say.

Slipping an enveloped from her bag, she gestured for a guard to take it in to him, then continued, "My attorney has copies of some of the pictures. I will make sure you die and rot in here."

Matheus was shocked. The pictures were hidden, then locked in secrecy. How could Nancy access them? When he looked up to explain she was already gone.

His heart sank. His only hope was Anthony. He wished Anthony would visit him. He was ready to give up anything for that visit.

The guard with the envelope came in smiling. The envelope was open, apparently searched. The guard was enjoying Matheus's discomfort. In a friendly tone he said, "It seems like everyone has suddenly realized that you're missing."

Handing Matheus the envelope, he continued, "Here, take this." Then he sing-songed, "You—have—mail!"

Matheus's spirits lifted a bit. Unfolding a letter, he quickly scanned the content. This was the final blow.

To the Immaculate University community:

Following the resignation of Dr. Matheus F. Gale, the Board of Trustees is pleased to announce the appointment of Dr. Anthony Hopkins as president of Immaculate University. We are confident that Immaculate University will flourish under his leadership.

Board of Trustees

The paper dropped from Matheus's hand.

The guard still seemed amused. Tugging Matheus's arm lightly, he guided the stunned man back to his cell.

Matheus did not resist.

L O V E

LOVE

The heart skips a beat.

That's true, it does!

When he is standing somewhere behind you—you're not even sure where, exactly—your neck is suddenly stiff, butt cheeks squeezed.

And you wait.

You wish you could gather at least enough wits to turn slightly and glance at him, but it's just not possible. It feels like there are strings tightly attached between you two, and if you dare to move, they'll snap, slapping you hard against the wall. I know this sounds bizarre, but trust me: this is one of the cutest feelings ever. If you have not yet experienced it, you have been denied this treat of Mother Nature.

Do you know the reason why it is different? It's just some amazing feeling, absolutely different. You feel it only for one person out of the whole crowd in your life. No one else can move even an inch inside or out of you, but even the mere presence of this special one shakes the common sense out of you, rewarding you with racing heartbeat, goose bumps, and flaming blushing cheeks.

This is truly ecstasy.

Let's feel the love. How would it be if the feelings are mutual? He does know what's going on, and he relishes the feat ahead of him. He just leans by the table, arms folded across his broad chest, legs idly crossed, a playful smirk dominating the whole image.

Her jitters are evident, and the spectacle is worth relishing. Imagine if he walks closer and slides his arms around her waist! She would melt in that embrace, giving away all her stress, enjoying the loving warmth that he provides.

So, what do you think? Like it? All right then, let me take you through a journey filled with love, joy, and care.

Brace yourselves because love is in the air!

LOVE FOREVER

Chapter 22: Ted

Ted Goldsmith had not been this nervous on his own wedding day.

He could actually hear the thumping of his heart. He had wiped his moist palms dozens of times, but to no avail.

Standing at the beginning of the path, he felt it would end in a glimpse, but it never seemed to end. Every eye was shifting between him and the other end. He thought of all those times when he had played deaf while she tried to convince him that this man was the one she wanted—all those times he could never even think of giving away his favorite daughter. But today he was dressed up in a new Reid & Taylor suit, walking down the aisle to give the man his Amanda.

This was never an easy decision, but one conversation on that terrible evening had changed everything. He could still hear the urgency in Brad's voice.

"Hey, Ted! I need to see you. It's important."

Ted was not too thrilled, but every time he heard or saw Brad, Amanda's baby face came in front of his eyes, secretly signaling him to be sweet. Seeing his sweetheart in love was a blessing, he realized. So he had responded casually after a pause. "Yeah, sure, come over."

Brad continued hesitantly. "Will it be possible for you to come over to Langone Medical Center?" After a pause—"It's about Amanda."

Amanda's name made Ted jump from his favorite recliner, where he had been reading the paper while drinking his evening beer.

"Please," Brad said, "just come—no questions."

"I'll be there," Ted said.

Within minutes he sat in the back of his Rolls Royce with his driver, Steve, racing through the streets. For once, he didn't complain when Steve pounded over bumps and potholes while racing around sharp curves. Normally Ted would roar over even a little bump. He loved this car even more than his partner, Becky—a fact she pointed out and complained over more than a few times. He would always respond something like, "You didn't cost me two million dollars; the car did." He liked to tease Becky, but he couldn't live without her

The car raced to the emergency-room entrance. Ted hurried inside where staff directed him to meet Brad in the Intensive Care Unit lounge.

"I'm not ready to be a granddad," Ted said, hoping nothing serious was going on, "at least until the wedding bells ring. Couldn't you be careful?"

But Brad had a serious expression. "Ted," he said quietly, fixing the older man's gaze with his own. "Amanda tried to commit suicide." Brad quickly continued before Ted could react. "She has been disturbed these last several weeks, but refused to talk about it. I tried asking a couple of times, but she always retreated to her usual silence."

Ted was genuinely worried now. He had always found associating with Brad difficult, because it meant losing Amanda to him, but seeing him so distressed, he could not help feeling sorry for him even as he worried about his daughter. "How did this happen?" he asked quietly.

"I found her unconscious in her apartment—" He paused. "She tried—well, she sliced her wrist."

Ted winced. He could not disguise his shock. He had known his Amanda to be a strong girl. He could not imagine what must have happened that led her to take such a drastic measure. What was more surprising was the fact that she did not even confide in Brad. They had accepted each other as soul mates. How could she not tell him?

His heart went out to Brad. He wondered what he must be going through. Being in a situation where you cannot protect your girl because she is too independent is always very frustrating, and he felt that Amanda had been unfair to this young man. No matter how much he had shown resistance, he always believed that Brad was the right one for her. Patting his shoulder, he guided him to the couch. "How is she now?"

"She is out of danger, but still unconscious." After thinking for a moment he said, "The watchman at her apartment had been saying something strange. I'll get back to him and ask." Then he fell silent, lost in thought.

When Amanda regained consciousness, Brad left Ted with her and went back to investigate, then returned with the horrific story of a visitor and activity which was unbelievable and absolutely unacceptable. Brad later had a conversation with Amanda in which she told him all the details. Ted admired him for his patience then and later for the strategy of getting even with that bastard. Brad had left no reason to be doubted.

Walking down the aisle with Amanda now, he admired Brad and wished he was twice lucky to have another son-in-law just like him for Miranda. She had been so excited about the whole wedding scene that even a blind person could not miss her impatience. Ted had seen her standing at the far end, but that was obviously not the right place for her, so she bounced over a hedge and landed on poor Danny, which was close to lethal. Ted crossed his fingers because a cat fight between his young twins was the last thing he wanted right then. But, hats off to Danny! He controlled his temper and managed to straighten himself, slowly setting his hair back to its erect position. Ted wondered what a funny style this was, but every young man was crazy about it, and his son was among the leading ones. For Ted, the hilarious part was that every one of them thought he was so good looking that every girl was checking him out. Looking at the performance, Ted veered from his track and almost tripped, but Amanda held him firmly.

Right across them Brad stood on the slightly elevated wedding stage. The cool evening breeze had to be shivering him inside.

But Brad stood broad and firm.

Chapter 23: Brad

The image of Ted looking baffled and his evident discomfort definitely felt good.

He could not help smiling at Ted's awkward gait. He knew how difficult it was for him to give away Amanda. He had wiped his forehead at least ten times in last thirty seconds. He had even tripped slightly, then stared at the ground so sternly that had it been a kid it would have started crying. Ted was genuinely uncomfortable, and Brad was relishing every moment of it. He knew very well that had it not been for that horrible situation, this would have been a tough bargain.

Brad had never imagined seeing Ted so upset. Seeing his love for Amanda had touched him deeply. He had lost all his composure. For a man as powerful as Ted, with nerves of steel, he had proven absolutely vulnerable, broken inside when he stood outside the operation theatre silently praying for her recovery. They had both stood there clueless and flabbergasted. Brad witnessed the act of a gentleman that day when Ted quietly swallowed that wretched news just to spare Amanda any embarrassment, then let Brad handle it all. Starting from confronting Amanda to her rehabilitation and finally getting even with Matheus, Ted had been a great support all along. But now it seemed that the old Ted had returned and was very uncomfortable. Brad loved the feeling.

Standing eight feet away, he already felt like a winner. This was like patiently winning a silent war of gestures, eye contacts, and disapprovals where in the end the defeated presents his beloved possession. When Ted tripped, Brad clenched his fists to control the burst of laughter. Ted looked child-like, but what struck Brad right now was the way Amanda took charge and supported him so no one could see his falter. This is what Brad had always loved about Amanda. She might have been a fragile introvert, but Brad knew that when need arose she would be right next to him.

The arrangement exhilarated Brad because of the fresh smell of the grass and the red roses all along the hedges. Amanda had always visualized the wedding in a beautiful garden with a wooden aisle sprinkled with petals. And she had done exactly the same. The wedding was arranged by the water in a park near Ted's New York estate, with the cool breeze of the evening air, chirping of the birds, and scent of roses.

He was only looking at the chemistry between Ted and Amanda when James poked him. "I hope you did take good rest after last night's blast. Tonight is even longer," James teased Brad, whispering in his ears. Brad had been a bit careful last night in the bachelor's party, but James had devoured booze like a maniac. Brad was sure he was still hung over, so he elbowed him in the stomach. James started to tease more, but his father had already given him a menacing look, so he laughed and moved back. By now Amanda and Ted had also reached the foot of the stage. Ted lifted her veil and pecked her cheek lightly. Amanda hugged him tightly in return and looked at Brad with large bright eyes. She obviously relished standing in the company of the two men she was madly in love with, in peace. Her joy was palpable.

Brad extended his hand, and Ted shifted Amanda's hand into his before moving back. When they stood facing each other, Brad saw for the first time that evening that Amanda looked breathtakingly beautiful. He had been so busy enjoying Ted's discomfort that he missed what an angelic reward he was getting for his patience. He knew the magic of the dusk added to the enchantment, but he knew she really was that beautiful.

The minister was chanting verses from the Bible, but Brad was lost in the wonder of the moment. He wished time would stop so he could tightly embrace Amanda and kiss her hard. She showed mischief in her smile, and Brad was ready to expect any surprise from now on.

Brad was looking at her when James nudged him, producing the ring from behind. James eyed him with mock sincerity and asked, "You do, right?" He displayed an artificial smile for the minister.

Brad realized it was the moment. Until now, panic had not struck him, but suddenly he realized that these two little words meant a great deal. If he said them, that meant everything would change. Standing under everyone's impatient gazes, Brad wanted to escape. Beads of sweat appeared on his forehead, and he felt the taste in his mouth go sour. In confusion, he looked around. Everywhere he gazed, he saw only impatience. Miranda eagerly waiting to see them kissing so she could squeal with joy. Amanda's second brother, Adam, fidgeted as if his nicotine level were low and he needed to refuel. Danny had his eyes locked on the sexy blonde in a skimpy pink dress, ready to target her with his charm. James was already restless behind him. Ted and Becky and his mom and dad were simply waiting for him to proceed. Brad's sister, Nancy, was squeezing her husband's hand in excitement. Just as Brad's eyes met hers, she nodded and mouthed a silent I do!

Finally his eyes met Ted's, and there he found serenity. It seemed that the tables had turned, and now Ted was enjoying the occasion. After some time, Ted gave Brad a reassuring smile, convincing him to relax and follow through on his commitment.

This was helpful.

The minister repeated, but this time very firmly, "Do you take Amanda to be your lawfully wedded wife, to have and to hold from this day forward, for better or for worse, for richer, for poorer, in sickness and in health, to love and to cherish?"

Brad looked into Amanda's eyes, and there he could find patience, reassurance, mischief, and—best of all—love.

She lightly squeezed his hand and waited for his response.

He loved her immensely. This was enough to stop thinking about anything else.

And then it came, just as peacefully as the flowers blossomed, and he said, "I do!"

Amanda's eyes welled with tears.

The rings were exchanged in a haze, and before the minister urged them, Brad scooped up Amanda and their lips locked.

The minister smiled.

Their lips parted when they heard the burst and they saw the sky lighting behind them. Miranda had arranged for amazing fireworks, which went on for a long time, but Brad and Amanda hardly saw them. They rushed down the aisle between all the giggles and thumbs up to where Brad's Porsche waited.

They zoomed to the hotel where the wedding suite awaited them.

Chapter 24: Amanda

Amanda was not surprised to see Brad's entourage at the hotel, warmly welcoming the couple.

They accompanied them on their way up the elevator, trading barely disguised perverted jokes, which Amanda simply ignored. When they arrived the twenty-eighth floor and the elevator opened, all the guys started humming, which eventually ended up to be a very melodious rendition of Enrique Iglesias's track "Finally found you."

Amanda was beginning to enjoy it all, and her excitement peaked when they opened the door to their suite. The room was decorated in white from lacy curtains to the plush carpet. The furniture was painted matte gold, an ensemble accented by three large beautiful bouquets—one on the table by the window, another at the foot of the bed, the last on center table. A basket of fruit rested next to the bottle of champagne in the two-seater dining area.

Amanda walked towards the couch where all the boys had made themselves very comfortable with their cans of beer, apparently settling in to watch sports on the room's HDTV, probably a rerun from no telling when. Placing her hands on her slender hips she looked at them quietly. In another two seconds she got everyone's attention. With a mischievous expression, she tilted her head towards the door, pointing them to leave. No one protested as they all got up and began to wrap up.

Ryan seemed to be the saddest, so he quietly said, "All right, Amanda, enjoy yourself." Tugging Brad's arm, he tried to walk him out with them.

Amanda immediately grabbed Brad's other arm and pulled him back. "You're not going anywhere today," Amanda ordered.

Ryan pulled Brad back and protested, "Not even nature can part us. We are born to stick together." With that he hugged Brad.

Amanda did her best to pull Brad out of Ryan's embrace as she replied, "Don't worry, Ryan—from now on I will do that for you."

"Noooooo," Ryan protested dramatically.

James stepped in, pronouncing, "We have lost our friend to a diva from paradise. Keep your peace, young man." This was James's turn to display his scenery-chewing theatrics.

Amanda hugged Brad immediately so no one could come near, and it worked.

To counter Amanda's efforts, Ryan and James collapsed on the couch and said, "We will not leave if Brad stays."

Amanda's final attempt paid off. She looked at Nick and pleaded, "Nick, please help me!"

Nick could definitely empathize with Brad as he had been through such a stage only a couple of months ago. It was after that that Brad had also made up his mind. Holding both the guys by their collars, he pulled them up and marched them towards the door. On his way out he said, "Be ready in an hour, love birds—we'll be here to pick you. I hope you do remember Ted has arranged a party."

"We will be ready," Amanda said, happily bouncing her way to the door with them. The moment they stepped out she gave them a bright smile and closed the door.

Locking the door, she turned slowly and leaned by it. Folding her arms, she surveyed Brad from head to toe. Moving slowly towards him, she commented, "I must say, you're a damn sexy piece."

Brad supported her play and faked a stutter. "Wha-wha-what do you mean?"

Amanda laughed dramatically and said, "What's the wildest you can imagine?"

Brad made a naïve expression and responded, "That you will slowly come near me."

Amanda walked slowly towards him.

"Then you'll push me on the couch."

Next, he was on the couch.

"Then you will take off your extra-long dress—I wonder why you girls waste so much cloth—and show me your voluptuous curves hidden under your sexy beige Marks & Spencer laced undergarments."

Amanda was impressed. Brad's skill at seeing through literally any fabric was remarkable. Removing her beloved gown she tossed it on the other couch and slowly stroked her beautiful curves. In her high heels, legs slightly apart, she stood right across from him and started playing with her thong.

"Are you scared?" she asked.

"Not yet," he responded in a child-like voice, "but I'll be dead scared if you do anything more."

"Really?!" Amanda moved forward and climbed on top of him, legs on each side.

Sucking his earlobe, she whispered, "What's the GDP of US gentle-man?"

Grabbing her tight Brad turned over. Climbing on top he gave every single detail of the Gs, the Ds and the Ps.

Brad gave her all the pleasure.

Chapter 25: Brad

Brad had considered himself "experienced," but this time, with his beloved Amanda, he experienced ecstasy in ways he never thought possible.

Dropping on top of him, Amanda played with his chest hair and waited for her breathing to normalize. When their bodies stabilized, Brad pulled her up and kissed her.

Lighting a cigarette, Brad drew deeply with his initial puffs while playing with Amanda's hair.

Amanda asked, "Don't you like my dress?"

"It's beautiful, baby," he replied, kissing her forehead.

"Then why did you say it's a waste of cloth?"

"I actually said that? Oh!" Brad was speechless.

"I spent all my energy in finding this dress, and you're calling it a waste." Amanda pouted her lips to show that she was supposedly upset.

This meant that she wanted some pampering, so Brad wrapped his arms around her, kissed her, and explained, "You know what? These long and creepy dresses are to show off in front of other girls. For us men, all you have to do is show up naked with a bottle of champagne. We love it." Brad knew how to make her laugh, and he just did.

Patting her cheek lightly, he said, "Let's get moving, or your warrior Ted will come over and shoot cannons at me."

Punching him playfully, Amanda countered, "Stop it! That's my dad you're talking about."

"Yeah, and he is *my* dad-in-law. So hypothetically speaking, I have more rights over him. *You* had no other options, but *I* chose *him* over all the other options." He thought dreamily about all those other options, but he knew Amanda was the best. But now she looked sad . . .

Hugging her, he inquired, "What happened, baby?"

She took some time and asked very quietly, "Do you regret it?"

Brad was silent. He wondered where it was going, but he preferred for her to continue.

"I know," she started, diverting his gaze, "that all of what, um, happened . . . well, it was unacceptable, and marrying me, even after knowing it all . . ." She fell silent, then sighed and looked directly into his eyes. "Well, it must have been a difficult decision."

Annoyed, he wondered why women seem only to think about the negative. He had to stop her from thinking this way, but he did not want to be harsh.

He lit another cigarette and took deep puffs to calm himself.

By now, Amanda was inpatient. "Say something."

Looking at her curled up on his lap with her head resting on his arm, he melted. The glowing red mark on her neck made him proud of himself. Kissing her forehead, he spoke very carefully. "I do not believe in regrets. You are here because I love you, regardless of anything."

Amanda was listening raptly.

"And I never want to talk about this ever again."

This was a command, and Amanda clearly understood that the debate was over. She nodded, then quietly rested her head on his chest.

They showered together and dressed in their evening outfits.

Amanda was in the final stage of her touch-up when the doorbell rang. The moment Brad opened the door, Ryan and James burst in and hugged him.

"Oh, we missed you sooooo much!" Ryan was absolutely in his imaginary character.

But before he could give any more performances, Nick handed him the car keys and ordered, "Go get the car ready; we're coming."

Ryan looked definitely up for more fun, but did not protest. On his way out he called out, imitating a female voice: "Braddy, I miss you, baby."

Brad recalled how long he'd known him, this guy was a lunatic, and that made him smile.

Chapter 26: Amanda

Ted had arranged the reception party in the garden, inviting a long A-list of influential people. Amanda accepted that many of the guests had come mainly to develop contacts, to enhance their networking.

David Stark Design and Production staged the event, and it proved truly marvelous. Stark had arranged the left wall to be decorated with gold- and silver-painted candles placed in wrought-iron candle stands. A screen in the middle of the wall alternated playing the clips of the wedding ceremonies of Ted & Becky and Brad & Amanda. Dining tables lined the length of the garden with white, matte gold, and rust-colored decoration. The crockery was white and gold-rimmed with gold and silver cutlery complementing it. The rust-colored napkin matched the gold glitter painted on the candles lighting the tables. The far corner accommodated two large artificial autumn trees sheltering a four-tiered wedding cake under its splendid colors of love. An aisle ran from the entrance to the foot of the cake, right through the middle of the decoration. A band played soft music to entertain the guests. The stunning view was out of this world!

When Amanda and Brad arrived, all the lights were turned off, so only the glow of the candles twinkled. Music stopped and a spotlight focused on Danny sitting next to the wedding cake. He started playing guitar, and the spotlight widened, bringing Adam and Miranda in its focus. Then came the best moment: when Adam started singing Amanda's favorite song, "I do it for you" by Brian Adams. Brad floated past Amanda and joined his best friend to pay tribute to the prettiest lady on her big day.

Lights kept illuminating gradually to the beat of the music, so by the time Brad and Adam finished the song, the arrangement was completely lit, and Amanda was surrounded by all her loved ones. With Ted & Becky on one side and Brad's parents on the other, she walked towards the cake.

Danny was the first one there to receive her and hug her. Trying to suppress his tears, he said, "Amanda, I never thought this would happen, but I already miss you."

This was enough to get her into tears. Quickly wiping them, she managed to say, "Don't make me cry; it took twenty minutes to apply the mascara."

Miranda was already sharpening her tools to comment on Amanda's outfit. "Why didn't you wear the pearl necklace we bought from Raymond? When will you get any fashion sense?"

Amanda loved her kid siblings.

Nancy already adored Amanda, and was there to rescue her. "But she looks good, doesn't she?"

Miranda looked at her from head to toe and passed her verdict: "No!"

This was the conversation stopper, and Amanda preferred not to be discussed anymore, so she quietly moved towards Danny, leaving the two to chat. Slipping her arm around his waist, she kissed his cheek and asked, "So who's the next target?"

Danny pointed his gaze towards a pretty young girl dressed in pink. Between gritted teeth he commented, "I wonder what she thinks of herself. I even made sure she saw me stepping out of my Camaro, but she hardly gave more than a glance."

Amanda almost laughed at his frustration. Squeezing him, she advised, "For a change, you've met a girl who wants to see a gentleman."

The advice was ignored as usual. Rolling his eyes, he replied, "As if I'm marrying her. By the way, if marriage is the criterion for maturity, then where would you rate those two?" He pointed at Brad and Adam, who were busy smoking and feasting their eyes on two scantily dressed ladies' voluptuous curves.

Not making any effort to hide her shock, she asked, wide-eyed, "You guys would never grow up, right?"

Danny tightened his grip around her shoulders and confided, "We would never, but make us fall in love and we'll move mountains for you." Checking out another pretty lady, Danny brightened and completed his thought. "That's the reason we make sure we don't fall in love."

Amanda punched his shoulder lovingly and hugged him.

Just then Miranda announced, "Ladies and gentlemen, may I please have your attention? My lovely sister and my true best friend, Amanda—" She turned to look around for her. When she spotted Amanda, she directly addressed her. "If you had looked good enough, I won't have to bother searching for you."

Amanda flew a kiss in her direction and said, "I love you, too."

Miranda started again. "So, as I was saying, my lovely sister—who is also my best friend—has planned to abandon me. In any other case, I would've protested because she is too dumb to survive without my guidance; but for the first time in her life, she has made a wise decision—"

Turning towards Brad she continued, "To tie knot with Brad. This is without doubt that Brad is the best guy for her. And Brad, you're lucky! She's a darling."

Next it was Nancy who took center stage. "To Brad and Amanda, may you have a beautiful life full of love." After some applause she remarked, "Now would you two come over and cut the cake? We're starving." And there was a round of laughter.

The band played lively music while the cake was cut, then all during dinner. The family went around accommodating the guests. When the four-course dinner was done, most of the guests departed. The closer ones settled into groups to chit-chat over generous pours of sherry. Amanda stopped by all the groups and conversed for the sake of hospitality. When she was about to approach the group of Brad's friends, Ryan's mischievous expression stopped her short. Retracing her footsteps, she headed towards the entrance of her house, providing the group with only a bright smile, which was welcome.

After Brad's parents departed, she noticed that Ted had disappeared. She had a fair idea where he could be found, so she headed straight to his study. Approaching the large oak door, she paused.

Her heart was racing.

She could not stand to see Ted upset, and this wedding had been a challenge for him. The resistance he had shown in letting go of her had touched her.

Knocking heavily at the door, she waited. After some seconds, Ted responded, and she opened the door.

Ted was sitting behind his large desk with his cigar dangling idly between his fingers. He looked stressed.

Amanda slipped inside and closed the door behind her. Looking at the corner behind the door, she recalled the times when she used to pull Brad inside the study and make out like teenagers.

Walking rapidly towards Ted, she smiled brightly and asked, "Why are you in here? Everyone was asking about you."

Ted beckoned her to come over. "Just needed some rest. How about you, quite excited—hmmm?"

Amanda leaned by the desk and responded, "Yeah, pretty much." Holding his hand, she looked into his eyes and asked, "Dad, are you happy? Do you like Brad?"

Ted gave her a warm smile and said, "If I didn't, do you think I'd give away my favorite daughter to him?"

Amanda's eyes welled with tears. She squeezed his hand in excitement and fumbled, "Oh dad I'm so happy. I was always worried that you didn't like him. I even tried to end my relationship with him, but—" After a pause, she spoke with emotion in her voice. "I love him too much."

Ted was visibly moved by this expression of her feelings. She knew that despite his awkward discomfort, this was still the best moment of his life. Seeing his baby taking the biggest decision of her life and having the confidence of owning it gave him absolute satisfaction.

He patted her hand and said, "It's the best thing for a father to hear that his child has attained what he or she has wished for, and it's ecstasy if the inevitable choice is embraced on both the sides." With a warm smile he said, "I'm at ecstasy!"

Amanda hugged him tight. Placing a huge kiss on his cheek, she showed her joy and exhilaration. The conversation she had dreaded turned out to be the best. She did not know whether to smile or cry. Tears were streaming down her cheeks, yet she broke into a smile.

They were in the middle of this emotional release when the door knocked. Ted answered and Brad entered. Looking at both of them in tears, he got perplexed. Before he could ask anything, Amanda leaped towards him and gave him the good news: "Dad loves you." She was so excited that nothing cold tamp her enthusiasm.

Brad just smiled knowingly, as if he'd never doubted it. Looking over her shoulder, he smiled and said, "Thank you, Ted."

"You're most welcome."

This was the most cherished moment of her day. The two men she was madly in love were at peace. Amanda was on cloud nine.

Brad slid his arm around her shoulder and, turning her around, addressed Ted. "Do you plan to move, or should I call for a carriage? Everyone out there is thinking you're also privately entertaining chicks like Danny."

This definitely gave Ted a reason to laugh. Dabbing his cigar into the ashtray, he stood up. Brad and Amanda moved aside to give him way, then slowly followed him as he headed towards the door.

When Ted was out of the room, Brad grabbed Amanda and, leaning her against the wall behind the door, began kissing her neck. With one of his hands behind her back and the other squeezing her breasts, they tongue wrestled.

They had lost track of time when they finally parted. Straightening her dress and tidying their hair when they stepped out, they gasped to see Ted waiting for them.

Obviously they did not have anything to say, so he began, "I could not go out alone, so I thought I would rather wait for you love birds."

Amanda was too embarrassed to look at any of them, so she quickly began walking towards the door. Ted winked at Brad, and they began following her.

Chapter 27: Brad

Back at the hotel, Brad came out of the restroom to find Amanda in obviously high spirits.

She had caught a glimpse of herself in the mirror, and had paused to admire the image. Twisting and turning for every possible angle, she could not stop admiring herself. She had to be sore from the intense activities of the whole day, but still she kept her heels on.

She flashed him a lively smile and resumed her self-admiration. The glow in her eyes was remarkable when she surveyed herself, slowly and sensually.

This was the confidence that Brad always loved in her, and which he had made every effort to restore. Approaching right behind her, he slipped his hands around her waist and sensually pulled her closer.

"Do you see how much I miss you?" he whispered in her ear.

Amanda clearly felt his hardness, but she played naïve. Making a baby face she looked at Brad in the mirror and asked, "Really? You do?"

He sensed her body reacting to what he was doing—her warmth, the flush of her face, the faint aroma of her arousal. She was in a playful mood. Bard had nothing to worry about. They had their whole life for each other.

Moving her hair to one side, he lightly touched his lips on her neck, breathing heavily.

Amanda relaxed and placed her head on his shoulder. Kissing her neck, he gradually unzipped her dress. When he glanced at the mirror, he could not stop himself from admiring her beauty.

Her dress was loosely hanging just around her shoulders while his hand pressed her stomach. Her dark wavy hair dangled idly on one shoulder. She closed her eyes, parted her lips, and moaned every time he sucked her neck. With one hand behind his neck and the other squeezing his hand, she looked an embodiment of magnificence.

It was time to proceed; he pulled her up and embraced her. Carrying her to the bed, he felt proud of being in love with Amanda and promised himself he would never let anyone hurt her ever again.

*   *   *

Later when Brad lit a cigarette, Amanda settled her head on his arm, dropping her arm across his chest and slipping a leg between his. Sensually trailing her lips on his neck, she whispered, "I love you."

Brad smiled and squeezed her.

Rising on her elbow, she looked at him excitedly and said, "I'm so happy and thrilled that Dad loves you, too."

Brad smiled at her excitement and replied, "Fathers love their daughters in a special way. It's not easy to give them away." Amanda was listening. "I guess I'd love mine even more."

Amanda flinched. "I don't want a daughter," she declared.

The coldness and detachment in her voice broke his heart. She suddenly tensed up, and distress showed on her face. She had travelled back in time and was again insecure.

Brad held her hand and kissed her wrist, which had healed, but the brutal marks remained. Embracing her protectively, he wrapped his legs around her.

"But I want a daughter, just as beautiful as you are," he teased.

"It won't be easy protecting her. I cannot stand to see her in pain," she protested.

"You don't have to worry. If any son-of-a-bitch tries coming near her, I'll kill him!"

"What if she had an accident and you didn't know?" she asked.

"Every father keeps a track of his children. It's just, they don't make it obvious," Brad said, kissing her neck.

Amanda relaxed somewhat after a while, when the realization settled.

Facing her directly, Brad stroked her hair. "Ted knew," he told her quietly. "He allowed me to handle it, though, because—" He smirked. "Well, he loves me."

Amanda was speechless. She hugged Brad and prepared for a satisfied sleep.

He watched her drift off. She had him now, him and Ted.

All her nightmares were over.

GREED

GREED

Everything has a limit—except desire.

Desire is the wish that you could have more and more, and you cannot find an end to it. Nothing is ever enough. Aiming to achieve something inaccessible and striving for it is certainly laudable, but breaking ethical and moral boundaries to fulfill your desires is not acceptable.

Such principles are not something that the world is going to decide, but they do come from Mother Nature.

By nature, we are never satisfied. Our needs keep growing with the flow of our granted wishes. What initially used to be our wish becomes our need, and this never-ending cycle keeps us revolving around that fascinating fireball, which keeps switching colors and holding our attention but, in reality, has nothing to offer us. It is the hallucination that this unknown entity gives us that drifts us into the world unknown, the world so beautiful that we convince ourselves to do anything to get, stay, and belong there forever. We even convince ourselves that we have the audacity and the stamina of going through anything to get there.

We try by hook or by crook and finally succeed in achieving it, but that begs the question: What next?

Does this complement us?

Can we carry the protocol that this stage deserves?

Are we still the same persons we were, or has this show transformed us, too? We do not ask ourselves these questions for very long because there is no turning back.

Catherine did this to herself. Her desire fueled her passion to leave her loved ones and struggle on the streets. She did not realize how this lust took away her self-esteem, her confidence and her very personality.

But nature did give her one chance.

The elimination of Matheus from the picture provided her a new opportunity to pursue a respectable life. Does Catherine avail herself of this opportunity?

Go ahead and explore what fate holds in store for Cathy!

THE DAWN

Chapter 28: Catherine

Ever since the day Catherine joined Immaculate University, it seemed that life had taken a direction towards hell.

But the worst part was that hell wasn't even demolishing her. The new sunlight of a new day brought much more harassment, disgust, and insult. After the unexpected events in the interview, Catherine felt that she had gotten herself stuck in quicksand where the more she tried to struggle for freedom, the more she was sucked in.

Matheus proved to be the most unbelievable person Catherine had ever met. He had many personalities, and he very conveniently switched between them. In the office he treated everyone with such utmost professionalism that no one could imagine that he had any inappropriate sexual activity, even for bodily needs. On the contrary, every time he called her for an unexpected meeting, Catherine would see his menacing self. She had observed that such meetings were not only restricted to one-on-one with her, but also the way with many of the women, irrespective of their ages and relationship statuses. All were required to see him whenever he wished. It was evident none of them wanted to go but had no option. They could not even discuss their pathetic situations. Living this nightmare was not only part of the unwritten job description, but it continued outside the job anywhere and anytime he wanted. No matter where she would be, a single phone call indicating his number meant Catherine had to be available.

She had always believed she had a special blessing from God. She knew that He would not see her suffer for a long time, and so it was. The sudden alarm scattered everyone like a whirlwind that day and, when the dust settled, the bad days were finally over.

It had been two weeks since Matheus got arrested after the much-awaited seminar. He had made everyone go crazy in its preparation. For him this was an effort to be taken to the end of the world, and it actually ended his world.

Catherine could not help but smile. Everyone was intensely busy that day with tasks demanding attention every second. They knew that whichever university got selected after the presentation would be visited by the accreditation team and, after their final report, the award would be presented. Matheus was bent upon getting this award. In his fervor he had not even considered others as humans.

Everything on the campus had been transformed. The process was at full swing when she joined, so this was how she got welcomed. The initial phase flew by. She hardly got any time to familiarize herself with the surroundings.

She did attempt to find out where Amanda was, but never got anything but a vague answer. At work, a majority of the people were full of praise for her. A few ladies spoke negatively about her, which was obviously tinged with jealousy. But overall the feedback was worrisome, admitting that Amanda was a great person to work with, but lately that she had seemed very upset until she suddenly disappeared. Catherine even visited her place and was informed that Amanda had moved out. This was strange. She clearly recalled the two times she interacted with her. It was as if the earth had swallowed her.

Catherine wondered if she had also been through a similar incident that led her to that stage. This seemed like a possibility. But what she wondered was where had Amanda gone. She simply could not be traced. Everyone said she was very courteous, but no one knew her more than that.

One time in the hallway she tried to persuade Emma to tell her about Amanda. She was about to say something when Sebastian appeared. The blood drained from Emma's face. Soon after, she was out of sight as well as out of reach—forever.

That evening Catherine received a call for an urgent meeting, while she was wrapping up to leave. Matheus had crossed all the limits of brutality. He had not done anything provocative, but rather had affronted her with his gestures, words, and looks. Before he allowed Catherine to leave, he said in a chilly whisper, "Mind your own business; Amanda is not yours."

Catherine's body had gone rigid. She could not breathe. She could not imagine how this petty thing could reach the highest office. In an effort to protest, she prepared to speak, but was immediately stopped by a slap. The blow was so sudden and so hard that Catherine lost her balance. In her disorientation, she gathered herself and staggered out of the office. She did not have any strength to face that demon. Stepping out of his office, she wished that this devil of a man would meet the most terrible fates, and that along with him it would diminish all his stooges.

Catherine had no idea that that was "the moment". She was not careful what she was wishing for, but surely she wanted this wish to be granted.

And it was.

Matheus's glass castle shattered, releasing uncountable souls. The wave of relief swept all over. The university underwent a pleasant transition. The feeling of being spied upon lifted, and interactions among the colleagues brightened. Things were finally moving toward the cliché happy ending, and this was heartily accepted.

Initially Catherine also found the liberty fascinating. The realization that she was not being watched and she would not be beaten up was in itself an ecstasy.

Weeks passed, and then a month.

The university was struggling to regain its lost credibility. Everyone stood by Dr. Anthony Hopkins to help him succeed. Anthony had a very different way of working. He always injected his military practices into the routine. That proved difficult for many, but gradually everyone accepted it. Catherine was no exception. Her visits to the higher office ended completely, but now she actually got to know what her real job was. Her competence was put to the test. Everyone was trying to run the race as fast as possible.

Catherine quickly realized that she did not possess the skills and knowledge to continue this job. Matheus had completely ignored that. In all the turmoil, she had never realized this. Now when she failed in delivering her duties, every single mistake was highlighted and talked about. The university was going through a "perform and retain your job" phase.

Catherine tried using the same technique, hoping to seduce her new boss, Anthony, but it seemed as if only money turned him on. He snubbed her badly, and since then Catherine's role as an employee of Immaculate University had been nothing more than a mule. She was moved from one place to another, yet nowhere could she prove herself.

Her job and also her life were on the hook now.

One night Catherine could not sleep. She could clearly see her life dwindling. She was going back to her previous financial straits. She knew that in her perplexity, rather than performing better, she was giving more and more chances for eyebrows to rise. She was especially concerned because initially many of her expenses had been taken care of by Matheus. Sure, she had not been anywhere near achieving her dream of living in Amanda's apartment, but she had started to grow accustomed to being financially comfortable. She suffered from whatever Matheus did to her, but at least he compensated her with all that money. He had seen her need and got what he wanted for his own by fulfilling hers. Lying in her bed now, Catherine was again wondering if she made the right wish. Things were not supposed to work out this way.

She desperately longed to have someone by her side. Loneliness was creeping up to her throat. She felt an invisible hand clenching her mouth, blocking her air. She desperately struggled, kicking the air around her. Pushing herself up, she began inhaling heavily. Hair damp with perspiration and limbs jelly-like, she stumbled out of the bed and ran towards the door.

Out in the hallway she lurched to Susan's door. She did not have much energy left to summon, but still she began slamming her hand flat on the door. In her dizziness, she could not hear anything, but still she kept trying.

She struggled until she passed out.

Chapter 29: Susan

The brass ring was only a stretch away.

She knew it would be hers at any moment. All she had to do was proceed toward it and reach.

But somehow this was not happening. She could not feel her weight at all. She wanted to move up and embrace that bright ornament that was the center of everyone's attention.

Everyone's attention!

The realization of having others around caused her to panic. She kept telling herself that she was alone there.

Don't worry, it's yours! Just go for it.

Believing her inner voice, Susan stretched her hand. She was halfway there when a loud *thud* stopped her. It was so thunderous that her heart leaped to her throat. In desperation, she turned to see what had caused it.

Inexplicably, a sea of people raced alongside her. Far behind, a huge blue-green ball bounced and rolled, squashing everyone who came in its way. Susan couldn't believe it. She screamed. It seemed that all of humanity was rushing to save their lives and the Earth rolled around, demolishing all.

She desperately needed to save her life.

When she turned around, everything had changed. The brass ring was nowhere in sight. Everyone was in a desert with wild wind blowing, brutally scratching their faces with the sand particles.

Susan tried to run fast, but her feet stuck in the sand. She fought to free herself, but sunk deeper. Sand was swallowing her. She struggled to pull her legs out, but they would not move.

Anything she tried to grab slipped from between her fingers.

She wanted to scream, but her voice choked.

Anyone she touched turned into blowing sand.

Thud!

Thud!

The huge ball was rolling towards her. In an instant it would crash on her, breaking her neck, crushing her ribs, splashing her blood, leaving pain and misery and the end of her.

Susan turned to face death and was horrified to see the killing ball inches from her face. The brutality of death slapped her hard, and the next moment everything went silent.

Susan lay panting on her bed.

Her heartbeat drummed her ears so hard that she could not hear anything else.

Drenched in perspiration, she waited for herself to calm down. Moments passed and so did her fear. Susan began to feel herself when suddenly came the final *thud,* jerking her off her bed.

This was real.

She did not know what to do.

Then came another and another and another. Looking around she could see neither the desert nor the people or the giant Earth.

It was a dream—a bad dream! she persuaded herself. When she convinced herself that it was not real, her attention went to the door.

It was undoubtedly her door.

With weak limbs she moved awkwardly to the door. Peeping through the keyhole, she could not see anyone.

Wondering who could have been there at this time, she walked back to her bed. Easing under the sheets, she slipped back into her uncomfortable sleep.

She needed this because life was not ready to cooperate.

Chapter 30: Catherine

The noises in the hallway woke Catherine up.

She had been on Susan's doorstep all night. When she opened her eyes, she saw Larry's kids towering over her, and one was busy doing something to her face. Pushing them away, she sat up. Before she could say anything, they ran away laughing, hitting high fives.

Catherine stumbled back to her apartment and closed the door. Weakly she made herself some coffee. She sipped it slowly, looking out the window. Everybody was busy with their lives. It felt amusing, seeing everyone rushing for something none actually wanted to do.

"Money can make you do anything," she murmured. She could tell from the sleepy faces of the children they would have loved an extra hour in bed. The stressed expressions on parents' faces openly testified that if they could get only one more chance, just one more chance, they would undo every part of this setup.

Her coffee finished, now it was time for her to become part of the herd outside. Leaving the mug on the window ledge, she walked casually to the washroom. Last night's turmoil had so cramped her muscles that now she found it difficult to walk. Stretching her arms, she encircled her sides until they cracked. Finally, her body responded.

She walked into the washroom and nearly freaked when she saw her reflection. Abstract lines marked her face. Taking a closer look, she realized that there was an attempt at making a thick mustache and beard. She knew exactly who had done it, and she wanted to get even with them soon. Realizing she did not have much time to waste, she quickly washed her face and got ready. Passing Larry's place on her way out, she promised herself she would have a final word with him about his boys.

While walking towards the bus stop, she wondered how she had made herself such a lonely person. Susan was always there for her when she needed her. She had supported her when she was broke. How could she forget that day when Susan divided her turkey sandwich and gave Catherine the bigger half, when she did not have a single idea where the next meal will come from?

Catherine realized her selfishness.

She felt disgusted.

How could she ignore that person who covered her when she was left naked and shattered? She had to visit Susan and tell her how sorry she was. Maybe this was how she could feel better.

The crowd at the bus stop was growing, but the bus was nowhere in sight. It would be a struggle squeezing into the bus, and she was prepared. She fixed her eyes on the horizon where the road emerged from the distance. Early morning sunlight always made the pavement glisten like a mirror. She really enjoyed looking at the vapors rising from the shimmering road.

The moment the red color appeared on the horizon the crowd began to surge forward. Catherine was geared up to take the first chance.

The huge container displaying oozing scarlet lips swayed along the lane, finally halting at the bus stop. The heat from the engine swept over all the waiting people. After the regular wait of five seconds, the automatic door hissed and parted. The air-conditioned rush of cool air welcomed the waiting lot. Everyone rushed to enter.

Catherine had a petite girl standing in front of her. She was a bit slow and seemed afraid to make any move. People were pouring into the bus, so in no time it would be full. Before that girl could do anything, Catherine pushed her aside and climbed aboard. The girl lost her balance and crashed to the pavement, but Catherine had no time for apologies. She had always believed that if you cannot do something, then you should be pushed aside.

When she turned back to check on the girl, she saw that all her belongings had scattered and she was desperately gathering them. Catherine did not mean for this to happen, but she could not deny fate. *This was to happen; only if you had been smarter things might have been different*, she thought to herself as she settled into her seat.

Public transport has its own rules and regulations. It will not hurry up, no matter what emergency befalls its passengers. Catherine was already late, but the bus stopped at every stop and squeezed in more and more people.

By the time she reached the university, Catherine was too exhausted to even work. Entering the building, she noticed that nobody was to be seen near the time clock. Both receptionists were slumped on their seats, hidden behind the counter. She hurried towards the machine and quickly placed her finger on the sensor for identification. After two seconds the machine loudly responded, *"Thank you!"*

She wondered why it had to make so much noise. "You don't need to say thank you," she mumbled sarcastically, imitating the machine.

She had not walked even half the hallway when she noticed Sebastian standing in the dim passageway towards Dr. Anthony's office. This was definitely not good news. Sebastian never gave her positive vibes. Dodging any eye contact, she hurried towards her department and quickly hid in her corner.

The day passed in its usual rush, and Catherine was waiting for it to be over. About half an hour before time to clock out, she was packed up to leave when Sebastian walked in.

Approaching Catherine, he spoke in his hollow voice. "The president wants to see you."

Her heart leaped. This was déjà vu.

Thoughts of the old days flooded back. Even back then, this statement scared the hell out of her, and the effect of that kind of statement persisted. Clutching her notepad and pencil, she quietly stood up to follow him.

At the office Sebastian paused and gestured for her to go ahead. Catherine stepped forward and gently knocked on the door. She did not hear any response, but she knew that she had to go in. This was the third time she had entered Dr. Anthony's office. She recalled the first time she came for the interview, how she was brimming with hopes and ambitions. Today nothing seemed the same.

Catherine stood across the desk, waiting for instructions.

Dr. Anthony was busy typing vigorously. Amid his activity he looked up and quickly said, "Please take a seat, Ms. Catherine."

Catherine sat stiffly in the nearest chair. Silence fell again, and the only sounds that could be heard were the clicking of the keyboard. Catherine waited patiently, silently praying.

Dr. Anthony finished his engagement and sat back. Looking straight ahead, he addressed her. "Ms. Catherine, I've received reports on your performance since I've occupied the office—" He broke off the statement and slowly looked at her.

Catherine was waiting, blank.

"And they are not good," he continued after a moment. Your supervisor feedback is below average, and your attendance record is unacceptable." Bending forward, he looked at her sympathetically and asked, "What do you have to say about it?"

Catherine could not find her voice to respond. All these things that he mentioned, she knew them already. Dr. Anthony was waiting. She wondered what he was thinking. She did not know how to defend herself.

After some moments of silence, Anthony spoke, "Ms. Catherine, how can you prove that you are an asset to the university—*if* you are given a chance." Catherine noticed the emphasis on *if*. Her mind was racing. She had to think what she was good at. In her frenzy, nothing came to mind.

Anthony seemed to sense the storm within her, so he leaned back as if to give her time to adjust her thoughts. Then he started looking at his monitor screen. He must have been waiting for her to give him some reason why she should retain her job.

So she gave him one.

When he finally looked back at her, his eyes went wide and his mouth dropped open at the sight of Catherine topless right in front of him. His face turned red, and he made no effort to control his temper. "Is that *all* you can do?!" he shouted.

Catherine was already shaking. In her puzzlement, she quickly began unbuttoning her business slacks. "I—I can do many other things."

She'd gone way over the limit.

He grabbed the papers on the desk and threw then in her face, yelling, "I tried to prompt you to start working because we are beginning lay-offs, and this is what you tell me you can do?"

Catherine was clueless as to what to do now. She sat still.

When Anthony did not receive anything from her, he stated, "Gather all your belongings from this place and leave. You are fired!"

Catherine knew she had ruined it completely. She had a chance to make things better and she let it slip away. In protest she said, "But you can't do it. It's unlawful."

Anthony looked at her with an amused smirk. "Oh really? And your activities with Matheus—with former President Gale—were lawful, right?"

Catherine was speechless. The intensity of the moment struck her then, and she felt a chill pass through her whole body.

Even her sight disgusted him, Anthony harshly ordered, "Get back into your clothes and leave. Don't bother to come to the university anymore." With that he returned his gaze to his computer screen.

Catherine slowly dressed and quietly left. Collecting all her belongings from her cubicle she silently left.

Nobody knew and nobody cared where she went.

*   *   *

Unlocking the door to her apartment, Catherine glanced at Susan's door. It was still closed. *She must be at work. I'll check on her later*, she thought.

The evening passed in discomfort. Catherine jerked at every movement outside. Finally she heard what she had been waiting for. Susan's key clicked open the lock and Catherine rushed to the door. Susan was almost halfway in when Catherine called her.

Acting reluctant, Susan stopped.

After an awkward silence Catherine spoke, "How are you?"

"I'm fine." Susan was evidently not interested in the conversation.

Catherine surveyed the alley slowly and continued, "How's work?"

"It's fine." Susan made every effort to look disinterested in Catherine.

Catherine knew she couldn't leave things this way. "Can I come in with you? I thought we'd have coffee."

Before Susan could respond, Catherine was right next to her, shoving her into her own apartment. Once inside, Susan sighed and began preparing coffee.

"You should go freshen up," Catherine urged her. "I'll watch the coffee."

She tried to sound cheerful.

Chapter 31: Susan

Susan silently went to the washroom and closed the door.

Looking at her reflection, she asked herself why she even allowed Catherine to enter her house. She replayed the memory of that day when Catherine pushed her out. She had been happy that day. It was her first day of the new job. She had been as excited as Catherine when she started her job. She expected her to be warm and welcoming.

Rather, Catherine's response was a cold, "What's your salary?" On hearing the amount, Catherine had laughed mockingly. Then she stood up and, with a casual wave of her hand, directed Susan to the door, saying, "I've got more important things to do, like taking rest. I need to look good because I make this much money in one evening."

Now Susan felt as if she had been slapped, and she felt the same way again, right there looking at herself in that murky reflection of the stained mirror. She wanted to go out and tell Catherine to leave immediately. She was gathering courage to do just that when the door knocked. Her heart leapt to her throat.

"Susie, when will you come out?" Catherine inquired, sounding "concerned."

Stepping out, Susan avoided eye contact with Catherine. Looking at the floor, she quietly said, "Please leave."

Catherine must have expected this. Acting as if she did not understand what was going on, she asked, "Is everything okay, Susie?"

Susan had enough of Catherine's pretention. It fueled her anger so much that she stared into her eyes and spoke between gritted teeth "Leave—my—place. I cannot stand an insensitive person like you for another second."

Catherine's face fell. All the brightness and excitement of old days drained, and fresh sorrow filled her eyes. Sniffing back tears, she turned and began to leave. She was speaking to herself. "I deserve it. No, I deserve even worse. I was so lost in my busy life that I did not realize my loved ones deserved better." Pausing in the middle of the room she turned and looked at Susan. Tears were running down her cheeks. What she spoke next came in a choked murmur:

"Susan, I came only to say I am sorry." And her voice broke.

Susan was perplexed. She did not understand what to do. Part of her could not forget what Catherine had done, but another part of her wanted to reach out and embrace her friend.

Catherine looked Susan in the face. Then looking at the floor, she quietly said, "You are right, Susie. I do not deserve forgiveness. But I wish you always to be happy."

With that she turned and left.

*   *   *

Back in her apartment Catherine tried to assess herself and figure out how to control her pace. It was just that she wanted to achieve more and more things in as little time as possible. In her frenzy she had not been considering any of her relationships worthy. She only wished she could do anything to make Susan realize how much she meant every word she said.

She was in the middle of her catharsis when the door knocked. She had not even moved from the place yet and the door clicked open.

In the doorway stood Susan, holding two mugs with steaming coffee.

*   *   *

"You forgot your coffee," Susan said so sweetly that Catherine grabbed her and hugged her tight. Coffee mugs held precariously, they cried in each other's embrace.

Settling down on the couch, Catherine held on to Susan's hand. She still seemed surprised that Susan had forgiven her. Maybe she really was realizing that she had been selfish and discourteous and was ready to pay any price to get back her friend.

Looking straight into her eyes, Catherine asked, "Susie, how can I pay for how I behaved all this time?"

Susan smiled. She was happy that Catherine came back. She had missed Catherine very much. She always enjoyed her adventurous nature and got to have amazing experiences with her.

Sure, Catherine had been carried away, but she was not a bad person. She clearly remembered that moment when this poor soul was being brutally treated. She had been through so much; if she had misbehaved, it was probably in reaction.

They remained silent for a long time.

Still clutching Susan's hand tight, Catherine seemed to be waiting for an answer. Susan rubbed her thumb on Catherine's fingers and lowered her eyes. She could feel the intensity of Catherine's feelings.

"There is only one way that I would forgive you," Susan replied with a hint of mischief in her voice.

Catherine was too emotional to catch it. Tears began streaming down her cheeks and her grip on Susan's hand tightened. Susan realized she had to control the situation so she brightened and raised her coffee. "Sip the coffee and never talk about this again." She finished her statement, grinning from ear to ear. With that she waited for Catherine to ease.

When Catherine finally loosened her grip, Susan relaxed. It seemed Catherine was beginning to realize that Susan was no longer upset about Catherine's past behavior. Slowly a smile curled up on Catherine's lips, and this time the twinkle in her eyes brightened the room. She was so excited that she was ready to talk to Susan the whole night. There were so many things to catch up.

Catherine inched near Susan and exclaimed, "I came over to your place last night. I kept knocking, but you shut me out."

So it was Catherine's knocking that caused her to wake up. "Oh, that was you! Actually, I was so deep into sleep that I thought maybe it was a dream."

"No worries. You have the right to reject me. After what I did to, you I could not even expect forgiveness." Catherine was clearly genuinely regretting her behavior.

Susan did not want this to start again, so to change the topic she asked, "So what brought you to my door at that hour of the night?"

Chapter 32: Catherine

Sadness overtook Catherine, and she replied with sorrow.

"Things have not been good at all."

She stared at her coffee. Moving her mug around and around, she stared at the liquid, trying to gather all the things that had happened. She could not pinpoint where to start. Susan already knew what Matheus made her do, but what had happened after his departure was definitely uncalled for.

Susan placed her hand on Catherine's knee and lovingly whispered, "You can talk about it."

Taking a deep breath, Catherine gathered herself and spoke. "Ever since Matheus left, things at work have gone from bad to worse. While I had taken a sigh of relief, I did not have any idea that God has more tests for me."

She realized that she could not tell Susan that she was proven less than competent and asked to leave. She had to think of something. After a pause, she finally stated, "Anthony wants to marry me."

Her statement generated exactly the same reaction she expected. Susan was so struck that she could not find her voice. Her mouth hung open, her eyes wide. She tried to speak something, but Catherine was quick to continue.

"I rejected him on his face and left. And before leaving his office, I told him that I quit the job, too." Looking into Susan's shocked face, she asked innocently, "I did the right thing—right?"

The news had sunk in by now, and Susan was prepared to answer. "You are much wiser than me. Whatever you did, I would stand by you."

Exhilarated, Catherine hugged Susan, spilling some of her coffee. The intimacy had continued for some time when it suddenly struck Susan and she asked in the embrace, "Sweetie, what will you do about your job now?"

This was the moment Catherine was waiting for. Putting up a show of depression, she forced two tears to the brim. Then sniffing them back, she spoke in a weak voice. "I'll go back."

Susan had to strain her ears to hear her, but when she did she reacted abruptly. "You are not going anywhere. I've lost a good friend once; I'm not gonna let it happen again."

Relief swept over Catherine. This was a sign that her situation still had a chance. Depression suddenly evaporated, and a renewed energy was pouring in, warming her body. Her cheeks blushed and tranquility settled. Holding Susan's hand, she looked in her eyes and spoke. "How could you be so forgiving? I don't think I can ever apologize enough for what I did."

Susan squeezed her hand and brightly said, "You can apologize only by not talking about it again." Then getting up, she continued, "Be ready tomorrow. I'll introduce you to my boss; I'm sure he'll be able to help." When she looked at Catherine, her eyes were wide open with disbelief. Lovingly she patted her cheek and said, "That's what friends are for, baby. Now take some rest; you need to look good tomorrow."

Catherine could not believe her ears. At that moment, she realized how little she knew Susan, and also how little they were alike. Susan was doing all this, expecting nothing but friendship in return. Catherine was so unfamiliar to this feeling that tears streamed down her cheeks, and she was holding Susan's hand tight.

Slowly she dropped to her knees and lowered her head, then began weeping. In her muffled voice, she kept repeating, "Please forgive me. Please forgive me. Please forgive me...."

Susan held Catherine by the shoulders and lifted her up. Dropping a light kiss on her cheek, she spoke in a heavy voice. "You do not have to seek forgiveness. What happened can't be undone, but we certainly can look at a better future." Squeezing both of her hands she continued, "And let's leave all these bad memories behind."

When Catherine finally smiled, Susan brightened. Picking up the mugs she casually said, "Sweetie, you better take some rest now. We'll leave by 8:30."

Catherine walked her to the door and stayed there until Susan closed hers. Susan was a true friend, she realized. She was so moved, she made a promise to herself:

She would never hurt her again.

*   *   *

The night passed very slowly. Catherine kept twisting and turning in her bed before finally falling asleep, which was broken quickly by her alarm. She was ready in no time, and by 8 o'clock she was waiting anxiously for Susan to knock on her door.

After what seemed like ages, the knock finally came. Catherine leaped to get it.

On the other side Susan stood, calm and radiant. Catherine realized that Susan was a beautiful woman. Her large eyes looked attractive with the slight touch of mascara, and her chestnut hair flowing down her shoulders gave her a vulnerable yet strong appearance. Her most attractive feature was her broad smile, which genuinely brightened her aura. This boosted Catherine's mood, too.

"Hey, all set?" Susan asked vibrantly.

Catherine did not want to spoil the morning with regrets, so she smiled back and responded, "More than ready for a new start."

With that both the ladies marched out.

They got on the bus that headed to the industrial area. The realization surprised Catherine—she had never bothered asking Susan where she worked. She had always been so full of herself that it never mattered where Susan worked or what she did. She told herself that she had to leave all this regret behind and make a brand new start with her first true friend, Susan.

After a tiring forty-five minutes the bus halted at the bus stop. After a fifteen-minute walk on the pavement they reached a garment factory.

Catherine's heart began sinking. The building had a huge gate that opened to a long passageway lined with massive pipes near the ceiling. The time clock was located immediately inside the gate. Susan stood in a queue to get her attendance registered. Catherine stood at a distance and waited. Susan kept giving her occasional smiles just to keep her from getting bored.

When Susan was done clocking in, she led Catherine through the passageway. After every ten steps a doorway opened into large halls set up with enormous machines. They passed the first two doors and paused in front of the third. Susan opened her bag and produced a black apron with a blue star sewed on its top left corner.

Catherine felt a pang of pain in her heart when she saw the star. The lobby of Immaculate University flashed in her mind. She quickly recovered, but realized that Susan was already giving her a skeptical look. Before Susan could say anything, Catherine smiled and gestured with a bow. "May we move," she asked, adding, "— mademoiselle?"

Susan smiled brightly and responded, "Sure, sweetheart!"

When they entered the third hall, Catherine noticed that majority of workers there were women. This was the packing department. At a distance of two steps each stood small tables and chairs. Most of the tables were occupied, and all the women were busy folding the clothes, then sliding them in cellophane wrappings.

Susan took one of the tables in the corner and dragged a vacant chair from a distance. When both of them settled, Susan extracted some clothes from the carton placed under her table and began folding the clothes with an effortless perfection.

Catherine had been so shut inside her shell the whole morning that she had not heard a word Susan said. Susan had been chattering ever since they settled in the bus. Catherine had been smiling every time Susan smiled, and on other occasions she pretended that she had been observing the surroundings. Now that they finally settled in, she had no other option but to listen to Susan and respond.

"It's not much fun, but I get enough to run my kitchen," Susan was saying.

Catherine smiled in response.

"When I began working here I found it very boring, but now I've learned the trick, and I can pack more than a hundred pieces by lunch." Gesturing towards a girl about their own age, Susan wrinkled her nose with distaste and whispered, "Martha over there is even faster."

Catherine tilted her head to look, and her mouth dropped open when she noticed the speed with which Martha worked. She looked more like a machine, and the results of her work looked perfect. Catherine could not work in that manner. She was mesmerized by the display.

Her concentration was broken by Susan. "Don't worry, honey. You'll learn this very fast. It seems tough in the beginning, but later it's just a piece of cake."

Catherine forced a smile and pretended to be calm while her heart thumped wildly. She did not want to do this degrading job. This was too low for her standards. In desperation, she began scanning the room restlessly.

Susan had been noticing Catherine's anxiety, so she tried her best to distract her. Surely she must understand how difficult it was for Catherine. Being in a strange environment is always uncomfortable.

When Catherine started shifting back and forth on her seat, she held her hand and spoke very quietly. "Calm down, sweetie. In an hour we'll take a break and I'll introduce you to our supervisor." When she got Catherine's complete attention, she continued, "He comes around that time. I'll take you to him and you can always woo him with your charm." Susan winked.

Catherine was puzzled. She wondered if wooing with charm was the same that Matheus required. Moving closer, she asked in whisper, "Woo with my charm?"

Susan smiled broadly and responded with the same secretive whisper. "Men are easy to convince, aren't they?"

Catherine understood what she meant. This piece of information grew her anxiety a lot. She was not sure if she wanted another Matheus. But now she had no other option but to wait and see what fate had planned for her.

The next hour passed in what seemed like ages. Susan had also stopped talking. Catherine waited patiently, memorizing everything she knew about garments. She flipped through her unprofessional resume and prepared herself for a probable interview. Her palms were wet, so she wiped them on her skirt constantly.

Finally the hour passed and Susan piled the stack of wrapped clothes. Pushing her chair back noisily, she began setting the stacks on the carton placed under her table. When she was done, she quickly skimmed through the stacks, counting the packages.

"Let's have some coffee now," Susan announced, picking up her bag.

Catherine quickly followed her lead and stood up. Leading her through the rows, Susan reached a door where she stopped to deliver her stacks of work.

Then they crossed the passage heading towards the blue-and-white sign announcing *Break Room*. On their way Susan peeped into an office, which was vacant at that point. Murmuring to herself, she began heading towards the break room. Susan's pace was unexpectedly fast. It took Catherine an extra effort to keep up.

Catherine was almost breathless when Susan suddenly stopped. Her gaze was fixed on a man who had just exited the break room and was walking towards them. He was probably in his early thirties. His belly bulged, giving his gait a very comical look because it jiggled with every step he took. His attire was very unimpressive. His beige trousers clashed with a tucked-in light-blue shirt. When he approached them, Catherine noticed that his shirt was so worn out that his collar frayed around the edge.

"What were you looking for in my office?" he spat the moment he paused in front of them.

Susan was caught off guard. She stuttered and fumbled a few words before her speech began to make any sense."I—I—no—no. I mean, I—I was… wanted to introduce you to my friend, Mr. Arden." She gestured towards Catherine.

He scanned Catherine from head to toe. This sent a wave of disgust through her. When he finally looked at her face, Catherine forced a smile, which was returned by a display of tobacco-stained teeth.

"Why is that so?" he asked Susan, keeping his gaze fixed on Catherine.

"She is looking for a job. She is a very competitive girl," Susan advocated.

"How can you say she is competitive? What has she done that is extraordinary?" His questions were directed to Susan, but his eyes would not leave Catherine's body.

Susan was speechless. She was apparently intimidated, so this was the time when Catherine had to take over.

Before Susan could say anything else, Catherine took charge and spoke up. "I would not mind describing my extraordinary achievements if we go into your office." Catherine gave him a smirk.

His eyes went wide open, and his smile broadened.

Extending her resume to him, Catherine said in a seductive tone, "This would tell you what I can do as expected, but I can do many of the *unexpected* jobs."

Getting her message, he took her resume and gestured for her to accompany him to his office. Walking behind him Catherine turned to give Susan thumbs-up. Susan responded with two thumbs up and a large smile.

When they reached the door, it displayed a name: *David Arden.*

He entered the office and barked, "Come on in."

Catherine entered and closed the door firmly behind her.

David turned, looking surprised.

Before he could say anything, Catherine locked the door and leaned against it. Her hands began playing with the top button of her blouse.

David recovered from the shock in seconds, then slowly sank into his seat.

Catherine naughtily chewed her lower lip and asked, "Would you like to see the ordinary or do you wanna go to heaven with the *extra* ordinary?"

David's excitement oozed out.

Slowly Catherine began unbuttoning her blouse. When she was halfway down, she dropped the blouse from her right shoulder.

David almost jumped at the sight. He was on the edge of his seat, trying very hard to control himself long enough to see the whole show.

Leaving her blouse that way, Catherine seductively unzipped her skirt and dropped it down. Her fleshy thighs and pink panties were a treat for the disgusting man who waited anxiously for Catherine to come closer. In the next twenty minutes Catherine got her new job.

When Catherine let herself out of David's office, she spotted Susan waiting in the break room on a seat where she could get a clear view of the office door. Twenty minutes had passed, and Susan looked like she was beginning to get worried.

Catherine looked around to orient herself with the place.

Susan quickly walked out of the break room and called Catherine. Catherine hurried towards her and hugged her tightly. She wrinkled her nose and sniffed at the telltale scents, but before she could point it out Catherine began narrating her "awesome" interview. She talked about how David had asked very decent questions, which seemed to surprise Susan. Still, she looked relieved that at least Catherine had at least secured a job.

Tugging Susan's arm into hers, Catherine began walking towards the exit.

Susan stopped her short and reminded her, "Babes, how can I leave right now? I still have the whole day to work."

Giving a bright smile, Catherine enjoyed informing her, "I requested that David let us leave early and, guess what? He agreed."

Susan blurted, "David?" Her eyes wide, she was making sure her shock was evident. Susan's feet were frozen on the spot.

Catherine was pushing her to leave when David came out of his office. Susan's gaze moved from Catherine to David. After a moment, he gestured for her to leave, so Susan followed Catherine to the exit.

While they headed towards the bus stop, Susan asked, "What did you say to him? This moron has been the most difficult thing to handle."

Catherine took a deep breath, "I didn't say anything. I guess my resume spoke enough to keep him quiet." This was enough to make Susan silent, too.

They continued walking in silence. Guilt struck Catherine for a while, but she recovered quickly because she finally accepted that she was not good at anything but selling her body. She had been tried and tested many times at the university, but she had never performed. Even a petty job of folding clothes seemed difficult to her, but seducing a man came naturally to her.

It was almost as if she were trained in the art.

Welcome back, Catherine Taylor!

Chapter 33: Catherine

Catherine joined Susan traveling to work the next day. Uncertainty and discomfort hung over her.

Susan tried to distract her, but when she did not receive any response she retreated to silence. At work, Catherine sat again in the same chair opposite Susan, watching her.

Just as the clock struck eleven, heavy footsteps entered the room. Dead silence followed.

Perplexed, Catherine followed Susan's wide-eyed gaze to see David standing right behind her. He looked different. He was exceptionally *well-dressed* for the environment, and the pungent odor of his perfume clearly suggested that he had probably taken a bath in it.

Every woman in the room seemed to be in a state of shock, waiting for what came next.

As David scanned the room, his temper rose. In fury, he shouted, "What's the matter? Have ya all seen a ghost?"

Everybody stared.

When there was no response, he continued even louder. "Then get back to work."

Everyone plunged into their tasks as if nothing had happened.

Turning to Catherine, David smiled and politely said, "You come along with me. I'll give you your job description."

Catherine stood up quietly and, lowering her head, spoke in a timid voice. "Please, sir."

Leading her out, David stared at every woman he passed. No one dared to raise her head.

Once they were in David's office, he closed the door and grabbed Catherine, then pushed her against the door. "Show me what else you can do," he hissed, trying to make it sound seductive.

Catherine had learned to handle men, and being a victim of Matheus had taught her grace, too. Even his wildest pleasures had a charm, and no matter how much she hated him then, she always appreciated him later. This was because he never forgot the compensation, and he very well knew Catherine's demand was money. But here standing against David, she had to make sure if she would be compensated well enough before giving away her assets.

The clock kept ticking, but Catherine did not make any move.

By now David's anxiety had gotten the best of him, so he squeezed Catherine's arms.

Flinching with pain, she blurted, "Ouch! That hurts, Dave."

The innocence in voice must have surprised him, because he immediately let her loose.

Still, just as quickly, he slipped his hands behind her hips and pulled her closer. "I haven't stopped thinking about you since you left yesterday." His bulging tummy served to block out a lot of what he wanted to express, so instead he begged. "You made me feel alive. Please gimme the same pleasure—*please*."

Catherine knew now what to do. Raising her arms behind his neck, she grabbed his hair tightly and tilted his head back. Then kissing his neck, she stroked his ear and whispered, "What's my job description?"

His grip around her waist tightened. "It's underway. Keep showing your talent."

Slowly detaching herself, she continued, "I don't believe in showing all my cards on the first call."

David was amused. Loosening his hold, he looked at her face. "Fair enough. Then how would you like it?"

Pushing him away, Catherine slowly walked towards the dirty couch placed under the window. Trailing her finger along its edge she looked at David.

David leaned against his desk. He seemed to enjoy this view.

Catherine straightened and went up to him. With her face inches away from him she mumbled, "Do I get a confirmation if I blow your mind away?"

"You bet!" David affirmed.

Catherine pulled him from the collar and led him to the window. Turning him over, she pushed him onto the couch. The moment he landed, Catherine pounced on him like a wild cat.

David covered is own mouth as if to quiet his moans of immense pleasure.

She gave him plenty of reasons to make noise.

Chapter 34: Susan

Outside, Susan wondered what David was doing to Catherine.

It bothered her that she had brought Catherine here, so if anything unpleasant happened she would be responsible. The lunch break was over, too, and there was no sign of Catherine. David did appear a couple of times, but unaccompanied.

When the day ended Susan waited for Catherine until the last bus to the city left, but she wasn't anywhere to be seen. With a heavy heart Susan climbed the bus and occupied the seat at the back. Weird thoughts haunted her, but she kept dismissing them. Silently, she began praying for Catherine. She had to find out where she could be, so she decided to call David's office phone the moment she reached home. This did help her in getting over her anxiety, and she sat looking out the window.

The bus halted at the spot and Susan got off. Hurrying to her home, she almost tripped over some children's toys on the pavement. As she entered her block, she was taken aback by the sight of lights in Catherine's apartment. In utter panic, she began running towards her building.

Reaching Catherine's door, she started banging.

Catherine opened the door after a long while.

By then Susan had grown very upset. She plunged inside, hugging Catherine. "Oh thank God you're fine. I was so worried."

Catherine remained stiff.

It took some time for Susan to realize this, and when she did she slowly moved. She searched Catherine's eyes. "What's up, honey? Are you okay?"

"Yeah." She sighed, then looked away. "What's gonna happen to me?" She started easing toward her bedroom. "And you should control your hysteria. People tend to rest after a tiring day of work. You can't just go around banging doors." By the end of her speech she was almost in bed with her back towards Susan.

This was a familiar tone. Realizing the situation, Susan quietly walked out the door and silently closed it.

Back in her apartment, she debated with herself over Catherine's attitude. She had heard this tone not very long ago. *But she could be stressed. After all, she had a conversation with David. This is enough to make a person go crazy.* She consoled herself for the treatment she had just put up with. *Catherine will be fine in the morning. We'll chat about it on our way to work.* It was already getting late, so Susan ate her dinner and headed straight to the bed.

The next morning Susan got ready and went straight to Catherine. There was no response when she knocked, so she rang the bell. After her third attempt, Catherine opened the door.

Susan was shocked to see that she had still been sleeping. "Why aren't you ready yet? It's getting late."

"You leave. I'll go after eleven," Catherine told her in her usual sleepy tone.

"Are you crazy?" Susan began to protest, but was cut short.

"Stop being a mother. I know what I am doing. I don't take dictations from any factory laborer." Without waiting for response, Catherine slammed the door.

The realization took a moment, but when it hit Susan, it did with intensity. Susan had not expected this again from Catherine—or at least so soon. Shattered, she walked down the alley and out under the open sky. Walking to the bus stop, she promised herself that she would never help anyone.

*   *   *

The following month gave Susan vivid glimpses of the real Catherine.

The superiority complex in her was almost tangible. Never even once did she display gratitude to Susan. If they would encounter each other in their hallway or in the factory, Catherine would hurry away.

If Catherine was seen around the factory at all, it was always with David. She had the job of exclusively assisting him, and she seemed to do it quite well. When they disappeared into the office, Catherine would not be seen for the rest of the day.

And whenever Susan attempted to get her attention, she was severely snubbed.

Chapter 35: Catherine

In the evening Catherine was tired of listening to David's pathetic jokes, and she could not wait to go back home.

Things had not been very good since she had left the university.

The encounters with Susan annoyed her, too. She did not like Susan because she was too dumb. She knew one thing, that if Susan had been in her place, she would never have introduced her anywhere. Catherine could not stand her for this reason. The real irony was that Susan expected her to be grateful. This was funny.

Catherine was busy in her catharsis when she realized that David was staring at her.

"Excuse me. Sorry. I didn't hear you. Guess I'm too tired."

"Oh. Does that mean you won't accompany me?" He looked disappointed.

Now what is this new problem? she wondered. "I'm sorry. I didn't hear you," she apologized.

"Oh, no problem. I was saying that my friend Thomas is throwing a party. I wanted to take you."

Catherine had been edgy the whole day, and she had no idea why, but this invitation served to improve her mood. The idea of meeting others seemed good. She had not attended any parties since she was a kid. She had heard that David was known for partying with an elite class. Rich people could help her make better connections.

Heartily accepting his invitation, she responded, "I'd love to, baby. Should I leave early today and get ready?"

David agreed to her suggestion.

He always agreed.

*   *   *

Catherine was picked up by David around seven. She saw Susan on her way out, but ignored her. The astonished look on Susan's face helped convince her that she was wily enough to win any battle.

Getting into the car, she flashed a smile to David and asked, "Where are we heading?"

Stroking her cheek, David began driving. Looking ahead, he spoke.

"You'll enjoy it. It's a hell of a party."

"But where is it?" she insisted.

"Wait, beautiful. You'll get to know soon." He reached over and scooped her bosom.

Catherine was annoyed by his evasiveness, but she controlled her temper. Silently she began looking ahead, too.

"Are you mad at me?" David asked with fake innocence.

Catherine smiled back and squeezed his hand. "Why would I be?" she responded with even more innocence. This served exactly what she wanted—to *shut David up!*

They reached the dirtiest part of the port, down in the old warehouse district.

Catherine gnashed her teeth for her stupidity. How could she expect anything classy from this good-for-nothing heel? She decided not to step out of the car into that stinky area.

Ships were tugging in and large barrels were being carried here and there. The sun was setting and work was almost wrapped up, so some grimy-looking kids from the neighboring areas gathered near the pier and slipped over the oil spilled on the wooden deck. They deliberately slipped so hard that they fell flat on their backs. In just a few attempts, all of them had successfully spoiled their clothes, and now their faces were also being streaked with black and brown colors. Their activities made Catherine feel sick.

A group of young men who had finished work stood near their car, staring at her overly revealed body. Catherine had specially worn her voluptuous dress so that she would attract men, but all her plans had drained away in this place, this gathering David had chosen to attend. She wondered if the men standing around were his friends. She certainly did not want to get intimate with any of those grimy men.

Ignoring their stares, she turned her head to look at David. He was looking at her, amused.

This was enough to flare her up. Without caring about anything anymore, she began yelling at him. "Is this your bloody surprise of a fun party? I should have expected such a juvenile choice from you. Can you ever think of anything classy? You are useless, not worth the time of a woman like me."

By the time she finished, David's expression had changed from amusement to surprise, then to shock and disappointment. It was the first time she had spoken to him about him. Her opinion appeared to hurt him.

Wincing through disappointment, he spoke quietly, "This is not where the party is." He pointed towards a yacht coming into the harbor. "We'll be picked by that yacht. That's the party—" After a pause, he added, "And the surprise."

Catherine wanted to bite her tongue. She wondered why she had to be so impatient. If she had only waited a few more minutes it would've been a much better scene.

She had to think of something fast to get hold of the situation. David was upset and he was showing it. Catherine tried to talk, but he seemed numb to anything she said. Squeezing his hand, she slipped onto his lap and kissed him hard. This was a treat for the children who had by now stopped playing and were enjoying the scene. David did not respond to any of her efforts. Catherine was bent upon convincing him because she knew that he would be introducing her to everyone on the yacht, so he had to feel good about her, too.

In desperation she muttered, "If you don't start talking to me—" She wondered what she could do. "Well, then, I'll take off my clothes right here, in front of everyone."

This made him chuckle. He tried suppressing it, but Catherine got her escape.

Smiling brightly, she locked lips with him and did not part until he completely relaxed. When their lips finally parted, the yacht was already tying off and extending a gang plank for them. The children's eyes were wide.

Adjusting her dress and stroking her fingers through her hair, Catherine stepped out of the car. By now the port was pretty much deserted except for small groups of people gathering in different places. Catherine was an absolute misfit for this place, but the floating heaven waiting for her seemed just the right ending. Her black body-hugging dress was ending right where her thighs started, and she deliberately wore red panties so that they would be noticed. Her deep neckline exposed a perfect cleavage that could attract any man.

She walked briskly ahead of David, swaying her hips dynamically. It served both her purposes; every now and then she tilted her head back and looked at David, assuring him that all this display was for him. At the same time, she kept flashing smiles to the men on board scrutinizing her. *I'm gonna nail it tonight!* she thought with determination.

When she reached the yacht one of the younger men standing near the gang plank stepped forward and extended his hand. Catherine took it happily and boarded. She deliberately raised her leg a few extra inches so that her dress would gather up. The predictable reaction came when all the younger men in the group began hooting. To show her concern, Catherine turned back to see where David was.

He was standing on the plank, evidently not comfortable with what was happening. Taking his hand Catherine pulled him in. Slipping her hand under his arm, she pecked his cheek and proudly surveyed the venue. The group of young men passed disgusted looks to David, and he got more and more uncomfortable.

Catherine could feel things working towards a better direction. To spice it up, she snuggled into David, who suddenly stiffened. This surely was not arousal, but rather tension. She could feel that David wanted to get away from the group of younger men. Avoiding their scrutinizing gazes, he tried edging from the crowd, but it seemed that friendly faces were hidden somewhere on the other side of them.

As they tried to work their way through that group, the man who had helped Catherine aboard blocked their way and directly addressed David. "Well well! Who do we have here?" Surveying David from head to toe, he began pacing slowly in front of him. "So did you win a lottery ticket to manage being allowed aboard?" he taunted David.

Catherine wondered what this was all about, but watched quietly. She had no intention of sparing David any embarrassment, so she waited for more. David was angry, but controlling himself.

The man addressing David was determined not to let him through. He served as a barrier between David and the entourage, none of whom dared to offer a clear path.

Winking his already twitching eye, David shifted his gaze to Catherine, who immediately responded with a broad smile. Everyone around stared in stunned silence and waited for what might come next.

Seconds ticked, but no one moved, and finally one of this man's friend spoke. "Hey, Rick. Give it up. Give the poor guy some space."

No taking his eyes off Catherine, Rick slowly walked past her, brushing his arm by hers.

Catherine was excited, but she controlled her emotions.

Slumping his shoulders, David walked to his friends. None of them reacted to the unpleasant scene that occurred a few seconds ago.

Gradually the party began to gain momentum. Music was loud and liquor was flowing. People were settling into likeminded groups, and fun and laughter took over. Everyone was enjoying the evening, but Catherine's anxiety did not allow her to concentrate. She focused on the other group. Their gait and attitude spoke of their wealth. They were all dressed casually, but still Catherine could sense that they were her target.

David was saying something to her but she did hear him. It was only when he tapped her arm that she realized she had been staring at Rick for a long time. She had been so engrossed that the party ambiance had totally vanished and Rick was the only figure who existed.

Rick had noticed too, so David was openly wondering what she was up to. Under David's questioning gaze, she felt very uncomfortable.

To avoid any explanation, she quickly excused herself to grab a drink. As she rushed towards the bar in frustration, she stumbled over something and fell flat on the wooden deck.

Embarrassed, she quickly gathered herself. She was struggling to her knees when someone grabbed her arm and pulled her up with a jerk. Catherine wondered why David was doing this, but when she encountered the performer of the act her, mouth fell open.

She was standing only inches away from Rick.

With her eyes wide, she held her breath and waited for what came next. Neither of them moved for some time. Then slowly Rick slipped his hand around her waist towards her back. Pulling her closer and trailed his nose down her neck. Catherine was already shivering with excitement. Reaching down the valley, he bit her hard and suddenly pushed her away.

Catherine was flabbergasted. She stared at Rick in disbelief, and in response he smirked. Sipping his margarita, he walked back to his friends.

Taking a glass of sherry, Catherine turned towards David and was struck by a fit of annoyance because all of them were staring at her. Clumsily she walked towards them. When she was right in front of David, he whispered for her to cover her cleavage.

Reflexively, Catherine looked down to see why. She blushed. The spot where Rick had bitten her was glowing leaving deep marks. To cover her discomfort, she spat, "Why? What is your problem?"

"What do you mean why?" David was shocked at her response.

All of David's friends looked away to avoid their exchange and act unconcerned.

"Yeah what is your problem? If you're not good enough to stand up for yourself, at least don't stop me." She stared at him for several seconds with disgust and finally spoke between gritted teeth: "Good for nothing."

David was shocked. His silence gave her the chance to make her next move, and she did not wait even another second. Turning on her heels, she sipped her sherry and swayed her voluptuous curves all the way to Rick. She was cheerfully welcomed by the whole group, and Rick pulled her onto his lap.

He openly groped with his hand and mouth on any part of Catherine he wanted. To Catherine, nothing about David seemed to matter at all. Catherine's evening was getting better and richer!

After about an hour the gang settled and produced the sacred powder. Rolling it into small unprofessional cigarettes they began puffing. Rick shoved his cigarette into Catherine's mouth and demanded her to smoke. Catherine knew she had to do anything he said because that was the only way she could be part of his company.

After a few puffs Catherine began to feel dizzy. Everything around her seemed blurry, or maybe jumbled, and she felt weightless. She tried to keep her head straight but it kept falling sideways. After some unsuccessful efforts, she gave up and leaned her head on Rick's shoulder.

She was losing consciousness.

Everything inside her was stirring wildly.

Nausea struck, and suddenly a wave of heat spread all over, culminating with a mouthful of warm liquid filling her mouth. Her throat burned and she oozed the liquid on Rick's shirt.

Rick pushed her away with disgust.

Sprawled on the wooden floor, she vomited. When her body temperature somehow dropped, a wave of chill wrapped her and she passed out.

Catherine jerked back to her senses when a splash of cold water hit her face. Inhaling heavily, she struggled to crawl away, which brought huge laughter. When she focused on the reaction she realized that it was Rick and his group who were enjoying her humiliation. Rick was standing right above her, holding a paper cup. He was shirtless, and his tanned muscular body shone in the evening sun. When he saw that Catherine was back to her senses, he threw the cup away and walked back to his couch.

Catherine was still on the floor, but Rick began enjoying the party. She knew David was watching, but he did not make any move. Avoiding his gaze, she struggled and managed to get back on her feet, but the sudden change got her head spinning, so she grabbed a chair nearby.

When she felt comparatively normal, she straightened up and clumsily walked towards Rick and his gang. With great effort, Catherine escaped some of the embarrassment to sit quietly in a vacant space on one of the couches. She stole another glance at David, who was still looking at her. When their eyes met, David gave her a sad look, then looked away, shaking his head. Catherine knew he was feeling sorry for her, and there was nothing she could do. She had the option of walking back to him, but when she thought critically, she felt that there was no more monetary gain with David.

He had used him up.

So getting through her catharsis, Catherine headed back to her new gang.

By now a couple of young women had joined the group, and everyone was engrossed in conversations. Catherine was not welcomed, but she stuck to the group anyway. She had nothing imperative to chip into the conversation, and the few times that she did manage to say something it was met with uncomfortable shrugs. After a few more attempts, she finally gave up and retired to one corner, waiting for the evening to end.

When the yacht finally reached port, Catherine's company began to disembark. This was disturbing. She knew she could not go back to David now, and being alone would be too embarrassing. She waited for Rick to invite her, but he didn't seem to be concerned. So Catherine made the move herself. Slipping her arms around Rick's waist, she asked innocently, "Are you gonna leave me alone?"

Pushing her away, Rick blurted, "What is wrong with you, bitch? Lemme get off."

Rick was too rude, but Catherine did not mind. She made an innocent face and said, "I was wondering if you could drop me at my place." Lowering her tone, she finished, "I'd like to offer you some coffee."

Rick picked up the signal immediately. Curling his lips into a wicked smile, he moved closer to Catherine. Spanking her butt hard, he said, "Let's do it, then."

Catherine knew she had hit the jackpot.

When they reached the cars, it came to Catherine's absolute delight that he owned a Maserati. All his other friends also owned fancy cars. Catherine got into the car and waited for Rick, who had stopped to talk to Chris. She noticed that while Rick was talking, Chris kept gazing at Catherine occasionally. Whatever Rick was telling him was surely amusing him. Their conversation continued for another minute. Then Rick came back to the car. Squeezing her thigh, Rick announced, "Lets head on for a rocking night."

To Catherine's amazement, the Maserati zoomed with unbelievable speed. Adrenaline rushed through her body. Everything seemed to disappear around them and, in a matter of seconds, they were at the Golden Gate. Rick came to a halt and turned to Catherine. Weaving his fingers through her hair, he asked, "Where do I go now?"

Catherine was so lost in the luxury that it took her some time to orient herself. When she looked around, she was struck by nostalgia. This was the same place she had passed, ten months ago, to drop off Amanda. In the matter of time, it was not much, but so much had happened since then. It felt that she had lived a whole life in those past ten months. All flashed through her memory.

Impatient now, Rick honked to get her attention. The loud sound shook Catherine.

Jolted back to the present, she squeaked, "What the fuck!"

Rick's offended expression stopped her short.

Trying to contain the situation, she began to cover up, but Rick cut her off. "Where do I drop you?"

"Ah, umm, near the bridge—Bay Bridge," she stuttered with embarrassment.

Rick's surprised expression openly explained his antipathy. It was clear that he did not think much good of that area, but he digested this and continued. "All right, then you have to guide me. I haven't been there before."

Catherine felt better. At least he was cooperating. After that their conversation revolved around the directions Catherine gave him.

When they finally reached her place, Rick scanned the area with disgust. The garbage Dumpster overflowed with trash, and some of the trash was scattered on the road. Teenage kids occupied their usual spot and were busy smoking. The loud sound of the Maserati's throttle attracted everyone's attention, all heads turning their direction.

Catherine so loved this attention that she did not want it to end. Rick was waiting for her to leave.

After a few hesitant seconds she spoke. "Would you like to come in?"

Rick had a constipated expression. He was hardly breathing. Taking a look around, he gave her an annoyed look which clearly meant, *Do you expect me to get out here?* Then he courteously replied, "No thanks. Maybe some other time."

Catherine could not let go of this chance. If he left he would never return, so she pleaded, "Just a cup of coffee and then you can go." Trailing her index finger down her cleavage she looked at him playfully.

She had given him nothing to lose, so he waited to see if she would do more, exactly what she needed him to do.

Leaning back, he spoke. "Hmm. So what else do I get?"

"Anything you ask for," she whispered, leaning closer.

The boys outside were watching the show with amusement. Rick saw them, too, so he must have thought it would be fun entertaining them. He grabbed her hair and slowly lowered her head. When she was inches away from his zipper, he stopped. "Lemme offer you some coffee before I come over."

Immediately Catherine unzipped his trousers and began her regular routine, showing off her expertise. Rick was certainly enjoying it.

When he was totally involved, Catherine suddenly stopped and moved back. Frustration was all over him.

Before he could say anything, Catherine unlocked the car and jumped out. "I guess you're ready for the coffee now," Catherine teased through the window.

She hurried into the building.

Chapter 36: Rick

So much for dumping her on her doorstep and making a fast exit from the stink of this area.

When he entered the building, he was too aroused to notice the shabby interior. Spotting Catherine, he rushed towards her. She had already unlocked her door and was waiting for him. She was actually starting to look pretty good but she presented him no challenge. In the episode ahead, Rick practically received everything on a platter. He was simply not attracted to her.

He intended to hurt her but she, on the contrary, was enjoying even his harshness.

This was surprising. He had deliberately been brutal, very unlike his usual style, but Catherine seemed to be very comfortable. He wondered what activities she had been engaging in to get to where nothing was too much for her.

Rick had not fancied anything about Catherine, except in how easily he could use her to humiliate David. Her immediate acceptance had turned him off initially, but David's anger fueled Rick's continued interactions with her. Her sudden change in attitude towards David amused him for some time, but later he began to feel disgusted when he realized how low-class she was.

And now here she was, willing to give and give up anything for some fleeting attention. Women like her would do anything, especially for money. This one was no different from Paula. In her lust for money, Paula had made his life a living hell, so he had disposed her. Now his aim was to rid the world of as many of these women as he could. He had gotten rid of one.

He wouldn't hesitate to do it again.

Catherine whispered lustily. "Let's do it."

Rick did not make a move.

She begged. "*Please.*"

Loosening his grip on her wrists, he replied, "If that's what you want."

Not waiting anymore Rick gave her what she wanted. *Now you deal with it, because you asked for it!* He thought to himself.

When they were done, Rick immediately began dressing.

Catherine lay sprawled on the bed, watching him. "Why don't you stay over?" she asked. "I had a great time. Don't you wanna try again?"

Rick acted very serious and did not respond.

"Are you all right?" Catherine now seemed concerned.

Faking a smile, he spoke. "It's getting late. I must leave."

Now Catherine appeared lost for words. Getting off the bed she wrapped the sheet around herself and slowly walked towards Rick. With lips inches away from his, she whispered, "I would let you go on one condition only."

Rick was listening.

"If you meet me again… soon."

She was trying to be very seductive, but Rick was not interested. He had done his part, and now her clock was ticking. He knew she was waiting for him to respond, so he smiled. Kissing her lips, he said, "I would love to see you again."

Catherine should have felt his hint of sarcasm, but if she did, she didn't show it. By then he was working his way towards the door. Catherine saw him to the door. He nodded and hurried out.

As he reached the building exit, he heard her call out. "Wait!"

But he made his escape, and disappeared into the night.

Chapter 37: Catherine

She walked back to the bed with revitalized energy. Life was beginning to look good. Finally life was paying her back for all the time that she had served.

She snuggled under the covers and replayed key moments with Rick in her mind. He had looked at her with deathly intensity. The wildness in his stare had aroused her more and more. She had not felt this way in a very long time. She had even forgotten how it felt to really have sex. Matheus was never sensitive to her feelings, so she had locked them somewhere inside her. Being with Rick and experiencing intensity was beautiful.

With this amazing thought she happily went to sleep.

The next morning, she woke up pretty late. She had made up her mind that she would not go back to David so, enjoying her laziness, she plunged back to sleep.

By midday she woke up again. Her body was hurting badly, and her head was spinning. Dragging herself out of the bed, she made herself a steaming cup of coffee. This was the only thing that could brighten her and evaporate her aches.

Her coffee did do wonders. Refreshed, she began thinking about Rick. She had to meet him. It was just afternoon, so he must be busy at work.

She settled in to wait for his call in the evening.

The time did not pass very easily. She kept checking the clock every minute. She replayed all the scenes of the previous day over and over in her mind. They definitely did exchange phone numbers.

It was late evening now, and she had done all the chores at home just to kill time. The sun had set, and people were returning home after their tedious routines. Still, there was no sign of Rick.

Catherine had waited enough, and now she could take it no more. With a racing heartbeat, she picked up her phone and dialed Rick's number. She waited until it rang ten times, then disconnected, hoping he would call back.

Another hour passed and Rick did not reply.

Anxiety overtook her. Picking up the phone, she dialed again and was rewarded with the same response. By now she was shaking wildly. This was not possible. Rick had said he would love to meet her again. In desperation, she began calling him over and over. He had to answer a call eventually, and she was ready to go till that point.

Well into the night, Rick could not be reached. Catherine was already feeling tired. Stress and frustration were eating her from inside. After a few more attempts she gave up and collapsed on the couch. Within moments, she passed out.

For three weeks she searched.

She called and called. She spent an entire day finding rides and searching for that pier where the yacht had moored. She exhausted her funds, taking taxis down there every night to linger, shivering in the chilly air, scanning the water. Some local youths started taunting her. Two men tried to lure her into one of the warehouses. A teenage boy tried to rob her one night, but she had less than a dollar on her.

Rick never existed, it seemed. All she had was a phone number, and it was a mobile, so the woman at the library helping her search online said no luck, it must be a burner phone.

The stress and lack of sleep got to her more and more each day. She couldn't sleep. She ached, and she worried herself sick. She had no job, no money, no prospects, no man.

No man.

Then just as she started to feel a bit better, she got really sick.

The sleeplessness turned to fever.

Then a rash appeared on her hands, gradually spreading to other parts of her body.

And her glands started swelling. He couldn't move her head, her neck in constant pain. She was having trouble swallowing, and for the first time in her life, she feared dying.

She needed to see a doctor, but she had no insurance, no place to go, no understanding of free clinics or Medicaid.

She knocked on Susan's door, again and again. She dragged herself out to the mailboxes, hoping Rick had stopped by, maybe left her a note. Susan's name was gone from her mailbox. She'd moved away, not telling where.

She hitchhiked until she got to Amanda's place, but the doorman said she'd moved away, and *no*, he couldn't give some stranger such as Catherine any information.

She spent the night on a bench, then struggled her way home after daylight. She slept all day and then some.

In the middle of the night, Catherine jolted to consciousness. She had a boiling feeling in the pit of her stomach, and her mouth was bitter. She pulled herself out of the couch. Her joints were so stiff she could barely move, worsened maybe by sleeping on the tiny couch for so long. Stumbling her way to the washroom, she bumped into the door hinge, hurting her head. That jerked her into her senses, but it brought with them excruciating pain.

In a haze she reached for the toilet and nearly immersed her head. Warm bitter liquid filled her lungs and rushed its way through her throat, bursting out of her mouth and nose. Catherine's limbs had stopped supporting her, and still her body kept demanding. With a gap of some seconds another burst of vomit came, and this took all the energy she had left.

Slowly Catherine lowered herself to the floor and carefully set her head down. Wiping her mouth with her hand, she tried to open her eyes wide. Her vision was blurring, and gradually it was fading. Catherine did not want to lose consciousness again.

She struggled to stay awake but some invisible hand clasped on her mouth slowly choking her.

She opened her mouth wide and tried to inhale deeply, but this led to another round of stinking vomit, after which she did not know where she was.

*   *   *

It was not the light that woke Catherine, but the pungent smell that engulfed her. She continued to feel weak. The smell was unbearable, and still she could not move. When she had lost consciousness, she fell on the disgusting liquid, which now stuck on her face.

Mustering all her energy, she pulled herself up. Holding the wash basin, she struggled to her feet. When she looked in the mirror, she could not recognize herself. Her eyes were swollen, and the liquid that had settled on her face was red.

She looked down and, to her amazement, there was blood on the floor. This made her dizzy, but she controlled it. She washed her face as much as she could and staggered out to her bed. Crawling onto it, she reached for her cellphone and began calling Rick.

As usual he did not respond so she texted him, telling her condition. She ended her message with, *I miss you, but please, I need help. I am sick, very sick.*

To her surprise her phone pinged within a minute, and the sender of the message was Rick. This did boost her morale a bit, but she had to question why he waited so long. With some enthusiasm she opened the message and was shocked to see that Rick has simply sent her a smiley in response to her bad news.

She was still perplexed when the phone pinged again. This message from Rick took Catherine's breath away:

I'm moving out of the country, and destroying this phone before I go. Don't try to find me.

She totally went numb, staring at the glow of her screen. *Please!* she wrote. *Why are you doing this? I need help.*

She waited, but got no response.

She waited some more.

Finally, she texted again. *Rick, I'm SICK!*

The phone pinged again. He did care. He would help. He wouldn't leave her alone.

I know, he said.

What? What do you mean?

Pause.

Rick? What do you mean?

I know you're sick, you bitch. Welcome to MY world.

She gripped the phone, and it pinged one last time. She stared at the screen, at the last words from Rick:

You've got HIV.

Aysha Ehsan

Growing up in a military family, Aysha Ehsan traveled and explored the whole of her native Pakistan. Still wondrously young, today she holds a Master's Degree in International Relations & Affairs from Karachi University. She is a writer who has worked as a journalist and broadcast anchor in Pakistan and the Middle East, taught at a Russian university in Dubai, and she merrily pursues her career in teaching in Dubai, United Arab Emirates. Her penchant for seeing, feeling, and understanding life's many underlying realities infuses how she lives as well as the stories she dares tell.

Find Aysha

Twitter: @AyshaEhsan1
Facebook: aysha.ehsan.3
GoodReads: Aysha Ehsan
Instagram: Aysha_Ehsan
LinkedIn: Aysha Ehsan + University Dubai

The Fresh Ink Group

Publishing
Free Memberships
Share & Read Free Stories, Essays, Articles
Free-Story Newsletter
Writing Contests

Books
E-books
Amazon Bookstore

Authors
Editors
Artists
Professionals
Publishing Services
Publisher Resources

Members' Websites
Members' Blogs
Social Media

www.FreshInkGroup.com

Email: info@FreshInkGroup.com

Twitter: @FreshInkGroup

Google+: Fresh Ink Group

Facebook.com/FreshInkGroup

LinkedIn: Fresh Ink Group

About.me/FreshInkGroup

PAPALA SKIES

By Stephen Geez

Chicago native Rochelle DuFortier likes to imagine the future, her world a series of picture postcards so vivid they sometimes seem real. When a foolish mistake at thirteen causes her mother's death, she's sent to a secluded Hawaiian valley, an outsider "haole-girl" among pidgin-speaking boys who hurl flaming papala spears under the full moon to summon her mother's spirit. After boarding school and a prestigious university back east, the ambitious young woman is torn between chasing new career opportunities, discovering her mother's heritage in a remote French village, and meeting obligations pulling her back to Hawaii.

On this island steeped in ancient mythology and modern superstition, Rochelle tests the possibility of sharing pieces of her life with those whose beliefs she barely understands and never intends to embrace. She dives the depths of a pristine coral lagoon, conceals bodies in a subterranean lava tube, and challenges the eruptions of a living volcano, even as she deciphers the truth about her mother's death and struggles to satisfy new debts born of old betrayals.

Papala Skies is the story of a young woman who makes all the right choices, only to find herself living an unexpected life. It is about the need to belong, and seeking one's own version of truth amid such differing cultures' responses to wrenching loss and abiding grief. It is about yearning for a sense of place, yet having to confront new ways to honor the love of family and friends.

Will Rochelle lose what matters most, or might she learn what the smart octopus already knows?

www.FreshInkGroup.com

ISBN: 978-1-936442-07-2

SLIVERS OF LIFE

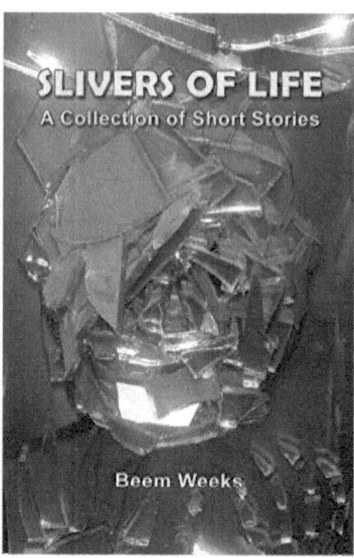

By Beem Weeks

These twenty short stories are a peek into individual lives caught up in spectacular moments in time. Children, teens, mothers, and the elderly each have stories to share.

Readers witness tragedy and fulfillment, love and hate, loss and renewal. Historical events become backdrops in the lives of ordinary people, those souls forgotten with the passage of time.

Beem Weeks tackles diverse issues running the gamut from Alzheimer's disease to civil rights, abandonment to abuse, from young love to the death of a child. Long-hidden secrets and notions of revenge unfold at the promptings of rich and realistic characters; plot lines often lead readers into strange and dark corners.

Within *Slivers of Life*, Weeks proves that everybody has a story to tell—and no two are ever exactly alike.

www.FreshInkGroup.com
ISBN: 978-1-936442-10-2

WHAT SARA SAW

By Stephen Geez

The boy looked back.

A simple pencil drawing, this depiction of a child watching from the reeds of a country pond frustrates and angers Geoffrey, unexpected reactions that stir Phrekka's lifelong passion for understanding the elusive power artists infuse in their creations.

Their only clue a "Sara" signature, the unemployed graphic designer persuades the enchanting Korean-American curator to help him discover more images by this enigmatic artist. From her world of privilege and mystical spiritualism to his of heartland farms and fundamentalist values, they will cross the country in search of the meaning in Sara's sketches, an odyssey to divine one extraordinary person's singular secret for touching people's souls.

Staggering revelations entangle them with issues of mortality and faith, sexuality and family violence, obligation and responsibility, deception and truth. Only by looking close at the dark and profane will they have any chance of coming together to create a legacy more beautiful than either ever imagined.

What Sara Saw paints exquisitely vivid portraits of two young people who must follow their hearts to recapture that innocent grace long lost to the whims of circumstance and fate.

www.FreshInkGroup.com

ISBN: 978-1-936442-03-4